MW01286158

A
SINGLE
SHOT

MICHAEL GRAYSON

Copyright © 2019 Michael Grayson
All rights reserved
First Edition

PAGE PUBLISHING, INC.
New York, NY

First originally published by Page Publishing, Inc. 2019

ISBN 978-1-64544-076-5 (Paperback)
ISBN 978-1-64544-077-2 (Digital)

Printed in the United States of America

Kodiak Alaska CGC Rush

If this ever becomes a book, I would like to dedicate it to two members of the US Coast Guard, Rodger Louibo, and Michael Zonon. Rodger was the best engineer I ever met. He often took time to pull us aside and teach us the engineering of the cutter *Rush*. I think he spent more time with me than the others as I was a little slow. When I made chief engineer on the cutter *Rush* during my second tour of duty on the ship, I took a strong interest in carrying on Rodger's tradition of training the new engineers. I knew the ship well from bow to stern, thanks to Rodger, and I loved it. As a ship took you through the many hellish places you were ordered to go, you fell in love with its warmth and protection. Back at the home port in San Francisco, Rodger was into fast cars and motorcycles. Rodger was not much of a ladies' man, although I'm sure he was being chased. Besides our time on the *Rush*, I had the misfortune of meeting my good friend in another hellhole, Port Clarence, Alaska, seventy miles north of Nome. Rodger had just married and was ordered to this frozen pit for a year of his life, just as I was completing my sentence. But the story of Port Clarence is a story for later on. Rodger, on returning home, was killed in a motorcycle accident. I never met his wife—maybe someday. I met my other dear friend, Michael Zonon—or Zoomer as we called him—when I was assigned to another horrible job on the Coast Guard cutter *Point Heyer*. I was serving as a boat chief at the time and it was Zoomer who helped me become a real Coast Guard chief. Zoomer, after retiring from twenty-seven years of duty, died from Lou Gehrig's disease. He was put to rest outside of the Golden Gate. I had asked my son to have the Coast Guard do the same with me when it would be my time to join my good friend. Although I do believe my transgressions during my life on the ocean will boil in destiny.

Chapter One

HIJACKED

On the bank of the Russian River on the Kenai Peninsula in Alaska stood Anna and her father, about thirty yards apart, fishing. It was late August, that time of year silver salmon ran up the river. Anna was an attractive twenty-two-year-old girl, but you couldn't tell with the waders, heavy jacket, and hat—normal fishing attire in Alaska. Suddenly, she got a bite, and the fish dragged the line as he swam behind a stump, then swam out again as Anna slightly tightened the line on her reel and began the fight. Anna had been here before. Sitting obediently behind her was her dog, Bodie. The same dog that had, many years before as a pup, swam into the water (like a Lab would do) and swam out into the river to break the fishing line, for which he was severely scolded. He learned his lesson after that and was now running and barking in excitement along the bank as Anna and her father fished.

Now Anna's pole was well bent over, meaning she had hooked a nice-sized silver. As she brought the fish along the bank, her father quickly netted the fish and pulled it from the water. At this point, they decided to call it a day and returned to her father's cabin on the other side of the river.

The cabin was conservative: two bedrooms and a nice living room with a woodburning stove and an over-the-top kitchen, a culinary delight. Dr. Eric White, retired now from medical practice, loved cooking. Anna's mother had died several years before, and she and her father had become very close, although Anna had been away a lot, attending Cal Poly University in California, where she recently graduated with a degree in biology.

Once at the cabin, they changed clothes and fishing attire to something more comfortable. While prepping the fish for dinner, Eric asked Anna, "Now that you have a college degree, what are your plans for the future?"

Anna replied, "I was going to tell you today but never got the chance. I applied for a position with the Federal Fisheries Agency here in Alaska and was accepted."

Eric smiled, thinking he would see his daughter more often with her working closer to home. During her time at Cal Poly, Eric missed her tremendously, so the prospect of her working closer to home was good news. Anna and her father spent the next two weeks together, fishing, shooting, kayaking, and just enjoying precious moments together.

After the two weeks passed, Anna began her training at the Federal Fisheries Agency in Anchorage. They taught her about different species of fish, but she was already on top of this. Her job, as explained to her, was to identify different species of fish and make a count of these fish. There had been a two-hundred-mile fishing limit imposed on Alaska by the United States due to other countries voyaging into Alaskan waters and, for lack of a better term, raping the sea. Anna's job would require that she be set aboard one of these fishing vessels, inspect the species and number to insure the vessel compliance with its United States permit. She was to be transferred on a weekly basis from vessel to vessel during the fishing season. She was trained on the operation of a two-way UHF radio, which only had a range of maybe a hundred miles. She was then helicoptered out over the Bering Sea and lowered onto the deck of the fishing vessel *Harassomaru*. She was a Korean vessel, about 180 feet but not much to look at. Anna went onto the bridge and met with the captain who spoke broken English, and as she soon found out, no one on board was any more fluent. She was shown to a small cabin below, where she saw a small bunk with a dirty mattress, no bathroom or facilities, and only two buckets: one for fresh water and the other to be thrown over the side. She later discovered a water faucet in the passageway outside her cabin for fresh water. She could see this would be no pleasure cruise. She took her meals with the twenty-two-man crew, who constantly stared at her. The food was terrible—mostly uncooked fish, sushi, you might say. Fortunately, she brought some of her own food and other supplies: sleeping bag and extra warm clothes to wear when working in the freezer where she would make her fish count.

In the morning, she went below deck to find the freezer where she began her count. She also went on deck to see the fish that were being brought on board and what was being thrown back. By the second day, she was convinced that this was all wrong. Her counts of cod and pollock were well above permissible numbers, and she had found large containers of Alaskan king crab and salmon that should have been thrown back as caught. In other words, they were taking everything and keeping it. She went back onto the bridge to confront the captain. The captain, she was sure, understood what she was telling him, but he blew her off. She thought by his expression that he was thinking, *Who is this girl, telling me how to fish?* With no satisfactory response from the captain, she went below to contemplate her next move.

Chapter Two

THE RUSH

We were going to go back about two weeks and move on to San Francisco, California, where the Coast Guard cutter *Rush* had been preparing for a two-month deployment in the Bering Sea of Alaska. The *Rush* was a beautiful 378-foot ship with a long cutter bow. She had two tall, black masts and her identifying red-and-blue stripes across her bow. She was an extremely maneuverable ship with many redundant systems, meaning if something broke, there was a backup system. The engineering plant had two Fairbanks Morse diesels that could move the ship along at nineteen knots and two Pratt & Whitney gas turbines that would move the ship along at thirty-two knots. She also had two variable pitch propellers. The designers and engineers got it right the first time. There was a small fleet of these ships homeported around the continental United States and one in Hawaii.

The *Rush* got underway using her bow thruster, an unusual piece of shipboard equipment for the early 1970s, which is a large electric motor with a shaft turning a propeller under the ship, hydraulically lowered and raised. The ship moved sideways into the middle of the Alameda Estuary, across from the famous Jack London Square where she was homeported. She engaged the diesels and moved slowly out into San Francisco Bay where she stopped to meet with a hovering Coast Guard helicopter. The ship was now in Helo Ops. This consisted of nearly twenty-five men on either side of the flight deck, with fire hoses and CO_2 to put out potential fires caused by a crash landing. Meanwhile, the helicopter landed into a wooden grid secured to the deck, locking its landing gear; the other dozen men quietly strapped the copter down. The LSO officer in charge of the landing on deck directed the crew by hand signals to release the helo as it took off again. These landings and takeoffs went on several more times. This was in the middle of the San Francisco Bay, flat-ass calm. In the Bering Sea, there could be no mistakes. The helo had to be downed and secured in a matter of seconds to avoid the next huge wave. Finally, the helicopter was secured on deck and refueled, another very careful operation. The *Rush* held 265,000 gallons of fuel, and any spark on board could mean the end of the 170-man crew and the *Rush* itself in the waters of the Bering Sea, where ocean temperatures drop below thirty-four degrees.

After all operations were completed, Captain Algrim told the officer of the deck to head the ship out the Golden Gate and proceed north as charted, to Alaska. She moved out under the beautiful Golden Gate Bridge and north through the Potato Patch, as it is known, off the Marin headlands, an area of none rough water. Its name was acquired from a vessel that sank there with a cargo of potatoes in the 1800s.

The trip to Alaska was about five days, if I remember correctly. I had made the trip thirteen times in my twenty-year-career in the Coast Guard, five years of off-and-on assignments aboard the *Rush* and one of her sister ships, the Coast Guard cutter *Midget*. I knew these vessels well. I had climbed their masts. I had the opportunity once when Captain Algrim called swim call several miles off the coast of Hawaii and jumped over the side. I swam to the bow of the *Rush* and stroked its bow in three miles deep of beautiful blue water. I was then told to get the hell out of the water by the men on deck standing shark watch with an M16 rifle. Apparently, we had visitors. I didn't have to be told twice.

I made chief engineer on the *Rush* many years later, from the time of this story in the early '70s, but I don't want this story to be about me. I was simply there or heard about things that happened.

The *Rush* was moving north and off the coast of Oregon, there was a strange-looking barge going south. The vessel was about 120 feet with a small wheelhouse on the stern. It was strange that a vessel like this, flying a Mexican flag, wasn't already noted and reported because the Coast Guard had numerous vessels patrolling off the West Coast on a regular basis.

The captain called for a boarding party to be assembled. This usually consisted of six heavily armed men with additional equipment as required. A vessel in question was often carefully measured and, if necessary, a bulkhead (wall of a ship) would be drilled and small borescope used to look inside the wall or tank, often revealing drugs. The *Rush* came alongside and ordered the vessel to stop, and with verbal prompting, she eventually did. A twenty-four-foot boat was sent across with the boarding party under the watchful eye of several men on deck behind a .50-caliber machine gun. Quickly, the boarding party came aboard from the portside stern, aiming shotguns loaded with double-odd buck rounds (very heavy shotgun loads). They moved quickly, securing the crew, at this point consisting of only four Hispanic gentlemen who didn't speak English or didn't want to in that moment. The boarding officer, after inspecting the vessel quickly, radioed back to the *Rush*:

"Captain, the vessel is secure. Four Hispanic men, and the vessel smells of marijuana everywhere. We have taken samples of the substances found on board. Sir, I think the vessel was laden with bales of marijuana that has been off-loaded up north. Sir, this vessel is sinking. The crew saw us coming and opened some valves that we have not been able to find. She is taking on water quickly!"

Captain Algrim said, "Secure our four friends and return to the *Rush*."

"Understood, sir!"

The *Rush* stayed in the area until the vessel sank well under and was headed for the bottom, as not to be a hazard to navigation. The Hispanic gentlemen were taken below and placed in a small lockable compartment with nothing in it, down by the gunner's mate's compartment.

The *Rush* continued on her way to Alaska.

Chapter Three

ANCHORAGE

I completed boot camp in Alameda, California, in January of '72 and wanted to stay in the San Francisco area, where I was born and had family and friends. But when offered the chance to attend an engineering school in York Town, Virginia, for a change in my life, I did something smart and took the school. This school involved training in gas turbine engines, hydraulics, and electrical systems. I completed the thirteen-week school, a very engaging and inspiring experience, which might explain why I graduated with a B+ average—way above my high school grades.

At this point, where our story really began, I returned to San Francisco for a week's leave and then off to my first assignment on the *Rush*, which was arriving in Anchorage. I asked for the *Rush* because it was homeported in San Francisco. What I didn't know was that just because the ship was homeported there, did not mean it would remain there. In fact, it was usually underway and rarely at home port. I was flown to Anchorage and found the ship. I would again say I regarded it as a strikingly beautiful vessel. When I stepped on board the gangway, I noticed I was walking down about four feet, but I could see the ship stood at least thirty feet above the waterline and forty feet at the bow. I reported in and was assigned a bunk and a locker and was told that in the morning I would be told my duties, but for now I was at liberty and free to go ashore. *This is my first time in Alaska*, I thought, *so why not?*

After some walking, I found myself in town and boldly walked into a noisy bar called the Ember Club. I had been a drinking man for my short twenty years and entered the club ready for a drink. My eyes adjusted to the dimmer light, and I saw a large man moving away from a barstool, brushing past me, obviously quite drunk. I saw an open barstool next to a very attractive blond girl. I quickly took the seat next to her and with some luck struck up a conversation with, I later found out, Caroline. I was and never had been a ladies' man or sweet talker, but when someone was nice, like Caroline, it came easy. Caroline was from Oregon and was a college student here in Alaska, working in the fishing processing and cannery plants. She would make very good money during the fish season and return to school with a lot in the bank. I later found out that some girls in Alaska made large sums of money in other ways. As Caroline and I were talking, she stopped me in midsentence and said that I must watch her friend Charlotte dance. Charlotte was sitting to the other side of Caroline, and we had barely been introduced when Charlotte stepped up onto a large horseshoe dance floor behind us and, with a very seductive music, began to dance and remove her clothing.

It was very tense between the coastguardsmen with their short hair and tidy uniforms and the locals with their more unkempt appearance, but everyone was having a good time. As Charlotte danced, men around the raised dance floor threw dollar bills at her, and if she came close enough, which she often did, they would shove a five down her panties. Soon, Charlotte had little left to take off, and the place was just going berserk. Then, suddenly, Charlotte pulled her panties down, exposing a penis. The whole place, from this unexpected insanity, went completely silent. Then the men around began grabbing for their money back before Charlotte could scoop it up.

After the barman got things under control again, I had to take a second look at Caroline; *No, this was all beautiful female.* Caroline and Charlotte, or whatever their real names were, left, and I realized I needed to find my new home. This was one of the nice things about the *Rush*. It didn't really matter where you were or in what port. No matter how drunk you were, it wasn't hard to find a big, white ship with two tall, black masts. When I found my way back to the ship, even with a few beers in me, it was obvious something had changed. The ship was now twenty feet higher, and the gangway was like climbing a ladder. The tides in the Cook Inlet, to say the least, were extreme.

The next morning, I was rudely awakened and told to report to the scullery (a small room near the kitchen) where I was to clean pots and pans for a month. I informed them that I was an engineer and should be working in the engine room, but that got me nothing more than a good laugh. The ship was getting underway, and once outside the Cook Inlet, I began to feel seasick for the first, and certainly not the last, time.

Chapter Four

THE STORM

The ship made way to Kodiak, Alaska, and tied up. We were met by some federal agents who took our four Hispanic gentlemen ashore. I know nothing more about what happened to them after that. The captain met with the admiral and was given his orders. We were quickly underway again and headed out into the Bering Sea. Our primary job, of course, was search and rescue when called upon. When not being called upon, we were to search fishing vessels from other countries, board them, and inspect its catch and numbers—very similar to what Agent Anna White was doing one vessel at a time. Except we could inspect a vessel every day or two and occasionally far more frequently. We had been underway about three weeks, and I was now working in the engine room and almost wanted to go back to the scullery because the engineering duties were tough. The captain came across the ship's speaker system, as he often did, to keep the crew informed of an upcoming difficult situation. And it turned out, we had one headed our way. The captain informed us that we had a large, fast-moving storm bearing down on us and that we would not be able to outrun it. He requested all chiefs and officers not on watch to be in the wardroom (officer lounge) in fifteen minutes. All hands were to secure the ship for very heavy seas. The helicopter blades were removed at this point and the copter well covered up. The aircraft and seawater don't get along well. All the hatches and scuttles normally open when underway were closed.

At this point, you had to call the damage control office and request to open a hatch so as to move around the ship. I learned later that normally the ship would run and hide behind one of the Aleutian Islands to take cover from high winds and tumultuous seas. In such circumstances, you were still in for a storm, but it was not as bad as being in the open sea. My job as a boot engineer was to help and learn from any engineering work taking place in the engine room or any of the other engineering areas. One of my other duties was to walk the ship and enter engineering spaces, taking readings and looking for problems. This watch was for four hours each day and night, every eight hours during dangerous times and every twelve hours when conditions were good. This was in addition to a normal eight-hour weekday. If you were also involved in Helo Ops, you were a sleep-deprived zombie. My next watch was the 12:00–4:00 a.m. shift (1200–0400 military time). Because of the storm, we doubled up watches, so two of us were making the rounds together. We walked through the engineering spaces, grabbing and holding onto rails and strapping onto hooks. The ship was moving so violently that your feet would leave the deck and, if not strapped down, you would be thrown against the bulkheads.

As my partner and I returned to the engine room control booth, a fifteen-by-twenty-five-foot room with hundreds of gauges constantly monitored by the throttleman and the chief engineer, to the surprise of us all, in came the captain. This was around 3:15 a.m. He also made his way down through the engine room to the control booth, holding on to the handrail while the ship tossed and pitched. Finally, the captain entered the control booth. The chief called, "Attaint-hut!"

"All hands, continue with your difficult duties," said the captain. He looked about and scanned the gauges. I think he knew what he was looking at, since he had a background in engineering.

Still holding onto the rail, the captain asked the chief about the failed reduction gear pump.

"Captain," the chief engineer replied, "as you should have been notified by the engineering officer that it is repaired and operational. With the movement of the ship, we strapped two men and the pump in place and bolted it in place, so it will function regardless of the ship's movement. Captain, we can work upside down." He paused, then said, "Captain, would you like a cup of coffee? It is a little different than the bridge coffee. There is a little diesel in it."

"Well, chief," replied the captain, "I will try that."

The chief poured the coffee, which the captain took black, and handed a cup to the captain. He took a sip and swallowed, then looked at the chief and said, "I think our diesel fuel needs a little bit more refinement."

"Yes, sir," said the engineer.

The captain made his way through the engine room—probably with a sour stomach from the coffee.

Meanwhile, the throttleman turned to the chief and asked, "Does the captain often come down to the engine room in the middle of the night?" The throttleman was new to the ship.

"You will be surprised where you see Captain Algrim," the chief answered, knowing the throttleman was new. "The captain loves his ship and crew."

Chapter Five

THE HOSHIZAKAMARU

When I got off watch, I found I couldn't sleep, which often happened. And that meant you were just a walking dead man. I called the bridge and requested to come up. The lieutenant said yes. By the feel of the ship, the storm was backing down a little. But to my surprise, when I had climbed to the bridge, I found the waves coming over the bow by ten feet, causing the ship to pitch and roll violently. The bridge of a ship was a fascinating place—all the electronics, the lights, the crew, and a view that went on for miles. You got an attachment or a love for your ship as it kept you safe and warm in whatever horrible environment you had been ordered to go into.

The captain came over the ship's speaker system a few hours later and said, "I'm proud of our ship and my crew, getting us through that difficult storm, but I need you all at your best once again. We have received a distress call from the Korean fishing vessel Hoshizakamaru. One of the ship's crew fell down one of the ship's ladders and is badly injured. Engine room, stand by for orders of flank speed on gas turbines. Helo pilots, report to the wardroom [officer's lounge]."

The fishing vessel was contacted and given instructions on when and how to receive the helicopter. One of the main points was that a helicopter built a great deal of static electricity, and the pickup basket shouldn't be touched until it was grounded to the deck of the vessel.

As the *Rush* began its encounter with the Korean vessel, I encountered for the first time a lifelong friend, Mark Mead, engineer on the helo. Mark and I would cross paths many times during our Coast Guard careers. We were soon making thirty-two knots through a sea so violent it jarred your teeth out. As we came within helo range, it was quickly launched, and we, of course, followed in case the aircraft went down. Mark later told me that once on scene, he opened the cabin door and began operating the winch to lower the pickup basket, and that his instructions must not have been passed to the crew because as soon as the basket came within reach, a crewman grabbed it and was thrown to the deck, probably pissing and shitting himself. I thought at this point we would be dealing with two medevacs. I saw the man get slowly to his feet as others put the man we had initially come after into the basket and strap him in. I could see they had completed the task and moved away, fearing what they saw of the first man touching the basket in the air. I winched the man up and pulled him through the cabin door and closed it. The man had a terrified look on his face. I didn't think he would have stayed in the basket if he had not been strapped in. We quickly flew back to the new location of the *Rush* and landed. I was there when the helo landed. I was part of the landing crew. My job was to be in a fire-retardant suit, and if there was a fire, I was to cut the seat belts if needed and assist the crew out of the helicopter. The helo was quickly secured to the deck, and the injured man still in the basket was taken to Michael in the corpsman's office. The *Rush* was now underway at full speed in the direction of the nearest port, Dutch Harbor. As we came within helo range, we again stopped and launched the helo. Michael, our corpsman, had done all he could to stabilize the man and make him more comfortable. Again, we followed the helo, and after it met with a medevac plane in Dutch Harbor, we once again retrieved our helo and crew. The captain decided to go into Dutch Harbor and anchor. Dutch Harbor was nothing like you saw on TV back in 1972. There was a small airstrip, a few shacks, no docks, a small store that mostly sold liquor, a bar called the Elbow Room, and of course the Russian Orthodox church from the 1800s, which I'm sure was not frequented often for prayer. After anchoring, some of the crew was allowed to go ashore. All cutters, as a standing order, kept at least a quarter of the crew aboard at all times. I was sure the captain was thinking, *Let's let some of the crew off the ship to blow off a little steam. What harm can they do here?* The small boats were lowered and used to shuttle the crew back and forth. Some of the crew walked around the island, but most of us found our way into the Elbow Room. On my first beer, I noticed six of the ship's chiefs sitting at a back table, and as I approached, I noticed a stupid grin on the senior chief's face. I then saw the same stupid grin move to Chief Hart's face, and the senior chief told me, "Grayson, you fucking worm, get away from this table."

I moved back to the bar as ordered and bought another beer. As I turned back, with beer in hand, I saw a young Inuit girl coming out from under the table where the chiefs were sitting. I will leave the rest to you. The sheriff walked into the bar. He was a man who looked to be right out of the 1800s—cowboy hat, long handlebar mustache, two .45 revolvers (ivory-handled, of course). I left the bar about midnight, with the sun still very high in the sky. You had to pay attention to time up there or you got all fouled up. On my way back to the ship, I, like most of the crew, stopped at the little store and picked up a bottle of bourbon to smuggle back on board. The captain and XO also came ashore and stopped into the little store for a few little things, certainly not liquor. Our friendly store owner made a point of thanking him for stopping in port and one of his best liquor sales in some time. Of course, before getting underway, the ship's officers and chiefs were standing by for a locker search. Thank you, store owner. Though the captain was likely planning this anyway. The little bottle cost me my fifty-dollar pay.

Hello Landing on Rush

Chapter Six

THE SEIZURE

We had been underway for about a weeklong fish inspections when there was a call about 4:00 a.m. (0400 hours). The bridge lieutenant knocked gently on the captain's cabin door. The captain answered the door, and the lieutenant explained that we had received a call but could make out only the word "Mayday!"

The captain asked, "Do we have the signal on the direction finder?"

The lieutenant answered, "Yes, sir, Northwest of us."

"Lieutenant, turn the ship in that direction at best diesel speed (nineteen knots) and have the engine room standing by with gas turbines. I will be on the bridge in ten minutes." He was on the bridge in five minutes.

As we slowly began to close the gap, the radio signal became clearer and finally clear enough to understand that a Federal Fisheries agent, Anna White, was in serious trouble. It was now about 5:15 a.m. (0515 hours) when we heard the whine of the gas turbines starting, and we all knew something big was happening. It wasn't long before the captain again came over the ship's speaker system, this time telling us about the Federal Fisheries agent needing assistance. He called for the helo pilots and all officers and chiefs not on watch to meet in the wardroom in ten minutes. The ship was alive like I had never seen. There were more than fifteen engineers in the engine

23

room control booth until the senior chief told us all to leave and that we would be called on as needed. I had friends on the bridge, radio, galley, you name it, and we all talked unless classified, so we had a good idea of what was going on even before the captain's briefing. We were now making thirty-two knots and had the suspect vessel on radar. The vessel was called on the radio many times in English and Korean and told to stop, but the calls were not answered, and the vessel did not stop. The captain had told the helo pilots to find the vessel and fly above and around so they would know we were there and, if fired on, to get the hell back to the *Rush*.

"I don't want a downed helicopter, so be careful, Commander," he'd warned.

We stopped briefly to launch the helo. The Koreans could clearly hear Agent White's call for help and tried to block the signal, but we had already set up alternate channels in anticipation of this. She radioed again with real fear in her voice, telling us that they were trying to break into her stateroom. She said after a minute that it went quite outside her stateroom and she could hear what sounded like a helicopter. The Korean captain knew he was in real trouble now and changed course directly west at full speed. There were no shots fired, and the helo returned to the *Rush*.

In the next briefing, the XO informed the captain of the course change and that the vessel was on course for Russian waters, where we all knew we, as a military vessel, couldn't go.

"At our present speed"—the XO went on—"we should intercept the vessel about ten miles outside of Russian waters, very close, but still in international waters."

The captain then said, "Commander, I want the helo up and watching from above, same as before. If shot at, return fire and get out of there. Chief Hart"—who was the gunner's mate chief—"I want two boarding parties port and starboard at the stern. Chief, you know the drill. Secure everyone and the vessel. Senior Chief, send over an engineer after all is secure to stop the main engine and maintain running generators for power."

We finally came within sight of the vessel and demanded them to stop. The captain called for Chief Hart again and told him on his command that he wanted the five-inch deck gun to fire a shell one thousand yards in front of the vessel. The captain himself called the vessel, demanding that they stop but was ignored once again. Chief Hart fired, but the shot missed, striking about two hundred yards off the vessel's bow. The explosion was incredible, throwing water high into the air and over the bow of the vessel. The *Rush* shook all the way down to its keel and felt like it moved back in the water two feet. The first time I had felt anything like that. I didn't know how our men in previous wars with much larger deck guns dealt with the sound and percussion.

The vessel continued on until Captain Algrim said over the radio, "The next one is going through your engine room." I didn't know if he was bluffing, but the vessel stopped.

We moved close alongside and quickly lowered a small board that maneuvered to the stern of the vessel under the watchful eye of two crews, forward and aft, behind .50-caliber machine guns. And guess who the senior chief selected as the engineer to go on board?

As we came alongside the vessel and threw rope ladders onto the hull of the ship with shotguns aimed above, we quickly climbed to the deck joining the party from the port side and began moving port and starboard up to the bridge. I was told to stay on the stern until called for. Our boarding parties moved to the bridge and down through the main passageway using plastic ziplock tied to secure all the crew's hands and feet. I was then escorted by one of our gunner's mates holding a shotgun. We still moved carefully and slowly to the bridge and down through the main ship's passageway where we moved past Chief Hart and others. There was an ax on the deck and obvious ax marks on the door. Chief Hart was calling out in a gentle voice, "Agent White, open the door. I am Chief Hart of United States Coast Guard vessel, the cutter *Rush*, and you are safe now. Anna, you are safe. We are going to take you back to the cutter *Rush*."

The gunner's mate and I moved on; we had a job to do. The gunner's mate checked the engine room again. I was to shut down the main engine, and that would be easy; from the looks of it, it wanted to stop on its own. The generators didn't look any better, but after inspection, I was able to keep them running until I was relieved and went back to the *Rush*. This was about the time two Russian MiG-35s showed up, flying low and threatening. The captain, as smart as he was, called Air Station Kodiak on an open frequency, telling them that we had a Korean fishing vessel in distress under tow to the nearest safe port. The captain lied a little for the benefit of the Russians. The MiGs left, no big deal. Agent White was taken to our corpsman, Michael. Michael would take care of our health, but much more importantly, he was someone you could talk to and he would really try to understand. Michael had the captain's ear without going through any chain of command. He would simply ask the captain if he had a minute, and the captain knew it would be more like a half hour but also something he needed to hear. Once, after a talk with Michael, the captain diverted the ship two hundred miles and airlifted a crew member home to be with a sick child.

Michael talked with Anna and determined she was not physically hurt but was in a mild state of shock. He gave her a light sedative and walked her up into one of the cabins of an officer who did not make the patrol. He laid her down to sleep and stayed with her, reading. The captain poked his nose in, and Michael gave him a thumbs-up. After an hour plus, Anna woke up, and Michael walked her up to the wardroom where some of the officers were finishing their evening meal. Michael asked to join them, but of course the reply was yes. The officers knew better than to bring up anything regarding the case. Some food was brought to them, and Anna thought to herself, *What a difference from that Korean vessel.*

After they finished a light dinner, another officer entered and went to them to explain that the Federal Fisheries Agency had been notified of the incident and that Anna was on leave until she wished to come back. The officer added that Anna's father had been notified of the incident and that she was safe aboard the *Rush* en route to Kodiak. Finally, he told Anna that her father was at the air station on the radio and offered for Anna to speak with him, which she gladly accepted. The three of them went up to the radio room (I didn't think Michael hardly left her side the whole time she was aboard). She had a brief, less than private conversation with her father. She asked the lieutenant when we would be in port. He said they would reach port in about five days but cautioned her not to state this over an open channel, adding that her father would already know this information as the crew at the air station had been notified. In fact, he continued, her father would be waiting in Kodiak upon their arrival.

We had the seized vessel in tow, stopping from time to time to relieve our crew and shuttle food across. The Korean crew probably ate better than they ever had, at least aboard a ship. We tied up in Kodiak with our seized vessel, which the state department quickly took control over, to negotiate with the Korean government to get their ship and crew back. The captain of the Korean vessel was going to be a visitor in the US for some time.

Meanwhile, Captain Algrim and Michael escorted Anna off the ship to meet with her father on the dock. After the hugs and kisses and introductions, Dr. White asked the captain and Michael to come to his cabin on the Kenai Peninsula for a fishing trip. We were tied up for three days, so I later found out that the invitation was accepted. So with a temporary reprieve from duty, I visited a fascinating club I had heard about called The Beach Comber. It was an old cruise ship, about five hundred feet from fore to aft, that had been thrown on shore about a quarter of a mile during the earthquake and tsunami in Alaska in the early 1960s. Some smart people got together, righted the ship, and concreted it in place. They dropped the gangway, and with its original all-wood bar and dance floor, it was a ready-made club. The staterooms were ready to rent, with a girl, for a price. It was a unique club to say the least. On the Kenai Peninsula, along the Russian River where this story started, stood Captain Algrim and Dr. Eric White, fishing.

Dr. White looked downstream and said to the captain, "I think we're going to have to catch all the fish this trip."

The captain looked downstream and saw Michael and Anna holding hands and not doing a lot of fishing. "I see what you mean, Eric."

Chapter Seven

THE POINT HEYER

The story should end here but didn't. I was going to jump ahead about ten years. I stayed in the Coast Guard, maybe the smartest thing I did in my life, and some years later and a second tour on the *Rush*, I made chief engineer. This might have had something to do with a little incentive from Senior Chief Tainter during my first tour on the *Rush*. I could never figure out whether he liked me or hated me, but he sure sent me to a lot of engineering schools. It would start with him pushing me up against a bulkhead and getting in my face, saying, "Grayson, you are not my first choice, but I have to send someone to advanced engineering school in Virginia. So and so broke his leg, so it's gotta be you. If you don't come back with at least a B+ average, you will spend the next two years in the bilges," and so on. Maybe he just didn't like having me around because I would make the grade, and then he would ship me out to another school. And these were not cheap schools: Pratt & Whitney gas turbines, Carrier air-conditioning, Fairbanks Morse diesel, and more. I found all these schools engaging, which probably explained why my grades were so much better than my earlier high school grades had been.

After making chief on the ship, as required, I was transferred to the cutter *Point Heyer*, an eighty-two-foot search and rescue boat out of San Francisco, Yerba Buena Island. The *Heyer* was a twelve-man crew, and I was in charge of the engineering department. I thought this was going to be a great job. I was wrong. Nobody called the Coast Guard on nice, calm days. Our first trip with the new chief on board was to go to Santa Barbara, in Central California, and take over the eighty-two's duties there while she went into the yard for some repairs. On the way down the coast, the lieutenant decided to pull in for the night in Morro Bay. It just so happened that my brother Bob lived not far away and was having a dinner party at his beautiful home. My new friend Zoomer and I attended. There were about twenty people, and after dinner, some of us stood around a nice firepit drinking some of Bob's excellent wine. The conversation began to slow, and Bob asked me to tell a Coast Guard story but keep it brief (he knew how I could go on at times). So I told an abbreviated story of a Federal Fisheries agent, Anna White. At the completion of the story, a girl from the other side of the dimly lit fire said, "That was me."

I chuckled, until she said something I could hardly believe. She named the Coast Guard cutter *Rush*, Captain Algrim, details no one could know after ten years, unless they had been there. Then I recognized the man holding her hand. It was our old ship medic, Michael. We caught up, and I soon learned that Anna and Michael had married, her father had died, they had moved back to San Louis Obispo where Michael grew up, and Anna had gone back to school. They had two children—a girl and a boy. Michael had retired from the Coast Guard as a chief corpsman (not an easy task to achieve at a corpsman's rate). He was still in the medical field and on Saturdays would volunteer to teach the local lifeguards paramedic skills. And this was how Michael and my brother Bob had met. Bob was a lifeguard, and to this day is still a water dog at age sixty. Ana went back to Cal Poly as a professor. With many visits over the years to Bob's, I would always stop by and see Michael and Anna, learning how their story developed over time.

Chapter Eight

ONE HUNDRED EIGHTY DEGREES

W hile in Santa Barbara, not much happened. We were only called out once to assist a disabled cabin cruiser in flat-ass water. We pulled it into port. The end. I wish more of our time in San Francisco had been that relaxed. Most experienced people I had talked to agreed that as you left southern waters and moved north up the West Coast, the conditions got worse. We completed our duty in Santa Barbara and headed north for the home port. About 3:00 a.m., the lieutenant and I had the watch on the bridge along with the navigator. I split the engineering watches with my other three men. The engineering watch wasn't much; most of the time, you were on the bridge and would go down to the engine room to check on the two 1710 Cummins diesels and one of the running Detroit generators. We were about fifteen miles off the coast of Big Sur, a mostly unpopulated mountainous area between Morro Bay and Monterey Bay. We were fighting a ten- to twelve-foot sea, not a pleasant ride. The lieutenant was on the helm steering the boat and asked me for the small wastebasket beside me on the deck. I handed it to him, and he promptly put half of his dinner into it and handed it back to me. I placed it back in its restraints. It wasn't long before the lieutenant requested the basket again, and as he handed it back to me, he said, "One hell of a way to make a living, isn't it, Chief?"

All I could say was, "Yes, sir." Now understand, the lieutenant wasn't prone to seasickness, but I sure was. Somehow, I was hanging in there that night. After a little while, the lieutenant asked me to take the helm while he went below for a few minutes. We were all cross-trained to take over each other's jobs. Hell, with my training as an engineer, I could almost navigate anyway. I took the helm, noting our course north and our speed, and at a glance, I could tell we were fifteen miles off the coast with three large contact ten miles to port on our radar screen.

After a few minutes, the navigator said, "Chief, I am going below to wake up the relief watch."

"Very well," I said, but I didn't mean it; this left me alone on the bridge. When I woke up, I didn't know how long I was out, but I quickly checked the radar screen. All was good, but I had turned the boat 180 degrees and was now heading south. I slowly brought the boat around and back onto our northerly course just as the navigator returned to the bridge. I was wide awake now. The navigator ran his plot and said, "Chief, something is wrong here. We made very little headway in that last half hour."

I said, "I think the sea conditions have gotten worse. Just log it accordingly."

Zoomer soon came to the bridge and relieved me. I went below to the cabin that the lieutenant and I shared. I found the lieutenant passed out in his bunk and bouncing around like a rag doll. I pushed him up on his bunk and secured him in place using the bunk seat belts and pillows. I felt his forehead and could tell he had a fever. I thought it best to let him sleep and address his condition in a few hours, closer to morning. I then moved across the small cabin and climbed into my bunk and belted myself in, first belt across my legs, then across my waist, and then across my chest, shoving pillows in where needed to make the straps tight. Even with all those straps, you would still bounce as the *Point Heyer* fought its way through the sea. I awoke as sunlight began to come through the portholes, and to my surprise, the lieutenant was not in his bunk but, as I later found out, was back on the bridge, where I brought him a morning cup of coffee. The lieutenant then he came aboard. He told us that he was the last of his class at the academy, and he would do his best to support the crew and the boat to do our job. It didn't take long to find out that he was number one when it came to taking care of our crew, boat, and duties.

We made our way back into San Francisco Bay and tied up at Yerba Buena Island. Most of the crew went home to family. I went home to my dog and friends. I had bought a house some thirty miles south of San Francisco, in Pacifica, where I grew up as a kid and now lived with my good friend Mark Mead, another Coastie.

Chapter Nine

YOU DIDN'T NEED
TO COME BACK

In the morning, I was playing with my dog and about to pop my first beer and go for a ride on my horse up at the stables, being we had two days off, when suddenly the phone rang and the two-days-off bubble burst again. It had been less than twelve hours, and we were being recalled again. You had two hours to respond, or you were in big trouble.

As we all returned to the boat, the lieutenant informed us of our upcoming mission. A forty-five-foot sailing boat (blow boats, as we called them) was on its way down from Canada and hit severe weather five hundred miles off the coast of San Francisco. The five-man crew, exhausted and unable to fight the seas, had called for assistance. The lieutenant, as he often did, asked for questions and comments. I was sure the lieutenant knew what I was about to say, but I brought it up anyway.

"Sir, the *Heyer* doesn't have the fuel capability to go a thousand miles." (The *Heyer* was a coastal boat and was never designed to travel such distances.) I brought this to the captain's attention and was told that we would go, and as soon as another cutter became available, we would be relieved.

These kinds of meetings were open to the whole crew, and my second-class engineer, Bob, said, "Chief, Lieutenant, what about securing six fifty-five-gallon drums to the stern of the boat with a hand pump?"

"Good idea, Bob," said the lieutenant. "Chief, it will be done, sir."

The crew did everything possible to prepare for the long deployment. Our cook knew just what to bring: a little soup, a lot of crackers, and cases of Otter Pops (if you don't remember this from when you were a kid, popsicles are great for rehydrating after you puke your guts out). We were out the Golden Gate, fueled up, and stocked up by noon. In theory, the *Heyer* could do twenty-eight knots but never got going that fast due to water and weather conditions. Nobody called the Coast Guard on a nice, flat, sunny day. Just outside the Gate, we began plowing through ten to twelve footers. About 10:15 a.m. the next morning, Zoomer, with a hot dog in his hand for an early lunch, I think just to make all of us on the bridge sick, picked up a broken radio signal from the sailing vessel *Breakout* on the UHF radio. The UHF single-side-band radio is a high frequency radio that can skip or bounce hundreds of miles across the open ocean but is no good inland where the low frequency VHF radio is used. With the sea state, we had made only 125 miles in the first twenty-four hours. In the next twenty-four, it was the same. It wasn't until the morning of the third day that we picked them up on radar some fifty miles off. The Pacific was being very ugly, throwing fifteen- to twenty-footers at us. It was noon when we finally had a visual on the stranded blow boat.

They had their sails down and were just bouncing about in a twenty-foot sea. Zoomer radioed them and told them the procedure for setting up a towline. Somehow, we managed to set up a towline as he explained, even amid raging winds and churning seas. We came close alongside and fired a line gun across their bow. (A line gun is a projectile with a small line attached. As the line is received, it is used to pull in a larger line and finally a one-inch nylon towline.) The *Breakout*'s crew managed to make the towline around the forward bow cleat, and we began to tighten the tow. All seemed well until the *Breakout* called, explaining that their hull speed was eight knots. If we towed them faster than their hulls speed, we risked dragging them under. This meant that at six knots, it would take us better than four days to reach San Francisco. The weather reports were showing no break in the weather, so Zoomer and the lieutenant decided to begin the refueling process during daylight and before we got too low on fuel in the tank.

We tethered Bob, being it was his idea, and he made his way to the stern of the boat as it jumped about on the choppy waters. He set the fuel line on deck and attached it to the hand pump and began cranking. After about fifteen minutes, Bob was exhausted, and we reeled him in only to leash the next man and the next, including myself, until all six drums were in the tank. We continued the slow tow and made hourly reports onto the Coast Guard group office, giving them our position and fuel condition. As we made our way under the Golden Gate, and what a beautiful place to be, the *Breakout* threw off the towline and motored up alongside, yelling, "Thank you, Coast Guard!"

I looked at the crew on deck, beat to shit and exhausted, and the words the lieutenant spoke a week before came to mind, "Hell of a way to make a living."

We went home and the *Heyer* went into a B-24 status for two days, meaning we didn't have to respond to a call for twenty-four hours and would stand down for the next two days. This meant a real two days off. When I was gone, my Coast Guard buddy Mark Mead would take care of my dog, Jerky, a pretty Irish setter. I had also bought a horse in Nevada from my friend and had her stabled in the back of the valley. You might say I was trying to have something of a normal life while being in the Coast Guard. Never happened.

I took Jerky up to the stables and saddled up my horse, Chaser. Chaser had a personality of her own. She stood only five hands (short for a horse), but she made up for it in spunk and smarts. I first rode Chaser in the desert outside of Dayton, Nevada, along the Carson River, with a friend. I was shooting jackrabbits as we rode. It was impressive that she would stand steady while I wheeled a shotgun about from her back. When we rode back to the ranch, Mary and I cleaned up the horses, and Mary informed me that she had a buyer coming to look at Chaser. I asked Mary how much she was asking, and she told me $500. I said, "Call them back and tell them she's already been sold."

Mary said, "Mike, you are in the Coast Guard. What the hell are you going to do with a horse?" Well, I sure didn't know it then. Chaser changed my life as much as the Coast Guard had done.

As Jerky, Chaser, and I left the stables, we began the long uphill climb to the crest of the hillside known as Sweeney's Ridge. From there, you could ride all across the ridgeline and up to the Crystal Springs Refuge, where no one was allowed. As a kid growing up, fences meant little to my friends and me, and we would often cross over into the refuge to fish the untouched San Andreas Lake. I knew these hills up and down the coast far better than most. But now, as a so-called responsible adult and a chief in the Coast Guard, I had to do things in a proper manner. So I looked into getting a permit to enter and ride through the refuge.

The first endorsement on my application was the Coast Guard Group Captain Carlson. Then I went to Captain Bourne of California Fish and Game and said that we had been doing joint operations outside the Golden Gate on the *Heyer*. I showed him the application as we were coming back into the bay that evening and asked him for his signature. I could tell he was very reluctant to sign, but seeing Captain Carlson's signature, he really had no choice. He signed, and then, in front of the lieutenant and others on the bridge, he said, "If you do anything wrong on the refuge, I will have you hung up by your boots." From the sneer on his face, I believed him.

The application required four signatures in total. Who was I going to get to sign next? Maybe the mayor of San Francisco or perhaps the governor? I decided to send in the application as it was, and within days, I received a badge to display, permitting two people to enter the refuge; a strict set of rules to follow; and a gate key to open gates, allowing access to the refuge.

As soon as the *Heyer* went into B-24 status, I set up a long ride with a friend from the stables. (A B-24 status meant the eighty-two-footer out of Bodega Bay, some thirty miles north of San Francisco, would cover our area and we would do the same for them in return.) My friend and I only got a few miles inside the gate when we were abruptly stopped at gunpoint. I showed the officer my badge and certainly mentioned Captain Bourne's name, which he obviously recognized. He asked where we intended to go, and I told him we were headed down to the lake to water the horses and then to ride past the caretaker's house (which I supposed he was) and finally out through the north tower gate. He asked how I knew my way around the refuge so well, and I didn't want to tell him I knew every road and trail of the refuge better than him from the time I'd spent there as when I was younger, so I simply told him that Captain Bourne had drawn me a map.

It was weeks later when in B-24 status that I took Jerky and Chaser out, with my pager just in case. We had just begun the climb out of the stables when a frantic man, who I recognized from the stables, came running down the hill, saying that his horse Maggie had stumbled on the narrow trail at the top of the ridge and fallen into the ravine, adding that he had been able to jump clear. I'll say it right now and get it out of the way—I didn't like him. He was black, but, hell, I didn't give a damn what color he was; it was the leather clothing, bright sequins, and large cowboy hat that turned me off from this wannabe cowboy. I knew the trail he had spoken of and rode Chaser to the beginning of it. It was obvious from all the broken brush where Maggie had fallen over, but she was nowhere in sight. I tied Jerky and Chaser off in a small shaded area and grabbed my canteen. I climbed down through the head-high brush, traversing several hundred yards, which took some time given the overgrowth and the steep grade. I started thinking that I needed to go back to Chaser and Jerky, when I spotted Maggie. She had obviously tumbled over the side several times end over end and likely got to her feet, shit-ass scared and breaking brush down the hill the only way she could go until she fell again off a twelve-foot rock embankment, finally landing on her back upside down and pinned in place by her saddle. I climbed down to her and carefully approached, so as not to get kicked. I pulled out my knife and carefully cut the saddle cinch strap, freeing her from the saddle. I then began pulling violently on her reins and yelling. She began kicking and jumping about until she was on her feet. I led her to a small twenty-by-twenty-yard clearing, surrounded by head-high brush. She was definitely in shock, but I guess instinct told her to lap up the water from my canteen that I had poured into a cupped hand to offer her. I knew there was nothing more I could do here. She wasn't going anywhere, and I needed to get back to Jerky and Chaser.

Jerky, Chaser, and I made our way back down to the stables, where Maggie's owner had stirred up quite a bit of excitement. Again, I'm going to say I didn't like this man, so from now on we'll just call him the Dummy. He was telling everyone who would listen how he tried to save his horse that had fallen over the hillside. I put Chaser in her stall and gave her a quick cowboy brush. Jerky and I found Bud, the owner of the stables, and told him that I had found Maggie but was uncertain what to do next. He said it was not on his stable's land and was not his problem. I called my good friend Mark Stewart (everyone knew him by the nickname he grew up by, Norton or Nort). I told Nort to take his chain saw and cut a hole up through the brush, following the bottom of the canyon until he found a small opening with a horse standing in it. I then called a veterinarian I knew, Bill. Now Bill, Dummy, and I listened to Nort's chain saw moving up through the canyon until it stopped. (Norton ended up getting shots for poison oak.) Bill, Dummy, and I made our way up through the hole that Nort had carved through the brush. Five hundred yards up, we came on Nort and Maggie. Bill went right to work and told us it was amazing she was not hurt any worse. He cleaned and medicated some cuts and gave her a shot to relax her. I had brought a sleeping bag, flashlight, and bottle of booze, planning to stay the night with Maggie. But since Dummy was there, I told him to stay with his own horse for the night. He looked at us and told us he'd never slept outside before. I gave him the flashlight and bottle of bourbon. He told us he didn't drink. Nort looked at him and said, "Start."

I went home exhausted, fed Jerky, ate a little myself, and began thinking about how to get Maggie off that hill. Mark walked in about that time, and I told him what had happened. As I was starting my second bourbon, Mark said, "It sounds to me like you need a helicopter, and I think I know where we can find one."

Sure as hell, Mark drove us out to the Coast Guard air station, located near the San Francisco Airport. We caught the station commander on his way going home and walked with him to his car, explaining the need for a helicopter. He immediately said no. But after a little more talking about the hundreds of people and numerous TV stations that would be there, he said as he drove off, "Okay, set it up with the Ops Center, but if anything goes wrong, I will have you two shipped off to the Arctic."

I thought better of telling him I'd already been there, but that was another story. Mark and I went up to the Ops Center and set up the flight for where and when and what was about to happen. About 10:00 a.m., Bill, Mark, and I began our way up through Nort's hole in the brush. When we got to the clearing, we found Dummy still wrapped up in the sleeping bag with an empty bottle of booze next to him. I kicked him awake, while Bill checked on Maggie. About that time, the helo came over the radio and was in sight. Bill gave Maggie another shot, and I walked her into the center of a cargo net. Mark called for the cable to be lowered, and as the hook came close, Dummy jumped for it, just as Mark and I yelled, "No!"

Dummy went to the ground shaking and pissing his pants (as mentioned earlier, the static electricity built up in a helo cable had to be grounded before it was touched). Now that the cable had been grounded (Dummy was good for something), Mark hooked the cable into the cargo net and radioed, "Lift away!"

You could not imagine the relief and euphoric feeling that came over me as I watched her carried two hundred yards in the air to be set down in the middle of the large horse arena, safe and sound. We grabbed our gear and quickly made our way down the hole. The helo was gone, Maggie was in her stall, and Bill was on his way to check on her. Dummy was in front of the cameras, telling them how he had spent the night with his injured horse and saved her life. Mark and I heard that and just walked away. Dummy died a few months later in a fishing accident, but if you ask me, that was no great loss.

Annie Gets a Lift

Tribune photo—R.A. Verdeckberg

to get back over the perpendicular face of
Rock in a cliff rescue training exercise last
t. gave commands to take-in or let-out the
xercise was conducted on a nearly straight
r their expertise in cliff-rescue operations
.

er District Leader
rns after Stroke

Regan, convalescing from a potentially
May 6 stroke, occupied his general manager's
onday night's meeting of the board of directors
th Coast County Water District, although direc-
oned him that night meetings were doubtfully
te for recovery.

from closely cropped hair and a 6-inch scar
n surgery, Regan showed little effect from the

d the directors that he was, with his doctor's per-
nd consent, coming to the water district office
Tribune Photo—R.A. Verdeckberg   utes on each business day and was scheduled
A horse plucked from its predicament orking four hours each day on June 10.

Things went back to seminormal for a while after that. We went up to Bodega Bay, about thirty miles north of San Francisco, to cover for the *Point Chico* (one of our sister boats) while it was in the yard for repairs. We got called out for a fishing boat that somehow lost its rudder. We towed her back in and all was good. Only, this skipper didn't just say "Thanks, Coast Guard," he meant it. That evening, he showed up at the station with two large albacore, and we had a great barbecue. This was the first time I had albacore; it was good, and he knew how to cook it. After about a week, we made our way back down the coast and back to our station at Yerba Buena Island. There was an alert that went out about a fishing boat out of Bodega Bay. Apparently, the skipper told his normal crew to stay home for several days and took several new deckhands aboard and got underway. One of the old crew called the Coast Guard explaining there was something funny going on with the fishing vessel *Water Dog*. The vessel went onto the suspect list. That meant, if seen, we were to stop it and board it with extreme caution. As luck would have it, we had tied up at Yerba Buena Island, and the *Chico* was leaving the San Francisco repair yard and going out the Gate when it spotted the *Water Dog* (which was later found laden with bales of marijuana). It was a job well done to make such a big bust, and we had just missed it.

Chapter Ten

MAD DOG

This next incident, I was very reluctant to tell because it had nothing to do with the Coast Guard, it had everything to do with me, and it was just plain ugly. My friends and family told me to tell it, so here we are.

On my many trips to the stables to see Chaser and get Jerky out of the yard and whenever the boat was in port, I noted this violent man at the stables, always yelling at his girlfriend about how to ride her horse around the arena. This man, I had observed, was a skilled rider but also a brutal man. I had to look up the word brutal to see if it was accurate: brute and especially cruel (and I added, a mad dog son of a bitch). He was a trick rider and would rope at his horse's mouth so hard he drew blood. On one Saturday morning, hoping not to be recalled to the boat, I went to the stables to take Chaser for a little ride. When I arrived, I saw a small crowd of people standing around the far edge of the arena, watching Mad Dog hitting his horse with his fist and grabbing her nose to shut off her oxygen until she would pass out and fall to the ground. Then he would kick her in the face until she would revive, and then he would hit her some more. The dozen people standing about watching said nothing. I saw Bud, the owner of the stables, nearby, and I said, "Bud, are you going to allow this?"

He looked at me and said, "Mike, let it go. This is called behind-the-barn training. It happens sometimes."

I walked back to the scene and just could not deal with what I was witnessing. From several yards away, I yelled to Mad Dog, "Hey, you need something to beat on, I'm standing right here."

He quickly made his way to me and commenced to beat the hell out of me. I thought I was a pretty tough guy. After blackening my eye, breaking my nose, and bruising me all over my body, he backed off, leaving me slumped on the ground against the arena fence. I later found out that he had been a boxer in the Marines. I collected myself and stumbled to my truck to make the three-mile drive home. I never made it. I was stopped by local police and told to return to the stables. Blood streaming down my face, I did as I was ordered. Upon arrival, I was handcuffed and placed into the back of the police car. I was yelling at the police to call a vet, and I would pay for it, but I got no response. I thought to myself, *What did I do wrong here? Was I supposed to just stand there like the rest of those sheep and do nothing?*

Then it got worse. The horse died, and everything changed. The police realized they had the wrong man in their car. I was released, and seeing there was nothing more I could do here, I finally went home and got cleaned up. I called the boat, and later the lieutenant, at home to explain what had happened. He said I should take the next two days to see a doctor, and he would call my reservist counterpart to stand in for me. It was the lieutenant's idea to train reserve personnel of the same rank and qualifications to take over and sail with the boat as needed. They sailed with us on many occasions, serving on numerous rescue calls.

I returned to the stables the following day to find that a veterinarian had been called by the Humane Society as part of an investigation into the death of the horse. The sheep and I were interviewed, and charges were brought against Mad Dog. The best part was, I was called to testify.

In court, I did the best I could to tell what happened with the bantering of Mad Dog's attorney and was quickly pushed out of the courtroom. I heard later that the sheep under the protection of the court had a lot of baaing to do. At the end, Mad Dog got six months in jail and was not allowed to own so much as a goldfish for six years. I went back to the boat and saw a doctor who had me snort cocaine and shoved what looked like a screw under my nose. After a few crunching sounds, he said, "It looks straight to me," and wrote a letter that I was exempt from any drug tests for the next month. Oh boy.

Chapter Eleven

THE PUERTO RICAN

It was about a week later, my face was going back to normal, and I just didn't need any more excitement in my life, when about two o'clock in the morning, Mark slammed my bedroom door open, yelling, "Your boat just called, and you've been recalled!"

I got up, dressed, and grabbed my underway bag with what I might need for a few days at sea and headed for the door, when I heard the phone ring again. Mark picked it up, and I stopped in my tracks, hoping it was a stand-down order. Mark put the phone down and looked at me. He said, "I've also been recalled." We both knew something big was happening.

I jumped into my Jaguar (yes, I had a nice Jaguar '67 XKE that did 140 miles per hour, and I had the speeding tickets to prove it) and headed to the boat, doing over one hundred when I could. I felt justified, and if stopped and put in jail, at least I wouldn't spend the next few weeks seasick. I arrived at the dock and could see that the boat had its engines started and was about to get underway. I ran down the dock and jumped on board. The lieutenant ordered all lines thrown off, and we raced away from the dock. I quickly made my way to the bridge because this was so unusual. The lieutenant had her at full tilt and said, "Glad you could make it, Chief," as he glanced over at me.

"I'm sorry, sir, I was detained by the Highway Patrol for doing 110 miles per hour in the 65 zone across the Bay Bridge."

He said, "I'll deal with that later. Right now, we have a ship on fire outside the Gate—and the XO and our second class had a car accident and will not be joining us this evening, so we are very shorthanded."

As we raced out under the Golden Gate Bridge, the six-hundred-foot ship came into view. The ship was called *The Puerto Rican*. It was ablaze below deck, forward of the superstructure, and the sides of the ship glowed bright red from the internal fire. There were two Coast Guard forty-foot boats spraying water on her sides but to no avail. I said to the lieutenant, "Those forty-footers aren't helping much, sir, and that ship could blow up at any time. Sir, I would have those boats back away."

He got on the radio and ordered the forties to back off and standby. The boats did as ordered, and minutes later, the sky lit up as if to make it daylight in San Francisco, a ball of flame reaching hundreds of feet high. Sometimes, I called it right.

Now I need to back up a little. I never read the Coast Guard investigation report and findings. I was just there. As we came on scene, the *Puerto Rican* was being towed out to sea from where it blew up, about a mile outside the Golden Gate. The way I saw it, the real hero was the captain of the tug. As I understood it, the tug was down the coast about five miles, working on the San Francisco swage out fall, when the captain heard the calls for help over the radio. He moved his tug up the five miles, found the ship on fire, and somehow got a tow cable across and began towing her out to sea. This would have been about when we arrived to watch her blow. Had this tug captain not done what he did, the ship could have easily lauded up against the Golden Gate Bridge when it blew, causing who knows how much damage. Instead, the ship was towed some thirty miles south, about ten miles off the town of Half Moon Bay where it was anchored. The lieutenant asked me, you might say a gentle order, to be airlifted onto the vessel and look for a lost man who was unaccounted for. So the Coast Guard helo that had been hovering overhead came close over the *Point Heyer* and lowered the basket that I got into and was lifted off the deck of the *Heyer*. I looked up to see my friend Mark on the winch looking down at me. This was one incredible ride. I was several hundred feet in the air and being blown about by the wind, and the basket was twisting and turning until I was set down on the deck of the *Puerto Rican*. I quickly unstrapped myself and rolled out of the basket, giving Mark in the helo the "All is well" sign. I moved very slowly down the deck of the ship and grabbed my radio to contact the *Heyer* to explain what I saw to the lieutenant, "Sir, the ship is still ablaze forward of the superstructure. The ship's deck half-inch steel has been folded back about two hundred feet, like a sardine can, and I can't move aft. Recommend the helo return and move me to the stern of the vessel."

The lieutenant came back and said, "Chief, the helo is on its way. Chief, you keep in constant contact and move with extreme caution."

"Understood, sir."

Mark came down with the basket. I strapped in and gave the "go" signal, and off I went. It was beginning to be fun. But understand, this was Mark talking to the pilot and copilot to direct this basket with me inside, and the pilots couldn't see where I was because I was under the helo, out of their sight. The helo team set me down perfectly on the stern of the vessel. I rolled out of the basket and gave the "go" sign. I again called the *Heyer* and told the lieutenant I was going to make my way below deck, "Again, Chief, use extreme caution," the lieutenant advised me.

As I started below, the visibility got worse due to the smoke and heat. I pulled my shirt up over my mouth and began yelling, hoping just to hear a reply. I was only down about thirty yards onto the first deck, and I could feel my lungs begin to burn. I quickly made my way back to the main deck, and as I stumbled out into the daylight and clean air, I found a Coast Guard officer standing in front of me. After coughing my guts out and clearing my eyes, I recognized the lieutenant from the *Point Chico* out of Bodega Bay (one of our sister boats). I gave him a quick rundown of what was going on and told him that after what I had seen below deck, I was sure that no one could be alive down there. He said, "Very well, Chief. Let's address the fire up forward."

We moved carefully forward to the front of the superstructure, and the lieutenant, looking like Columbus pointing out at the still raging fire, was saying we could put fire pumps here and fight the fire. I happened to look down at his feet as he stood in front of me and noted that as the ship moved with the sea, the water on deck would also move, and as it did, it boiled, meaning a hot fire right below deck. I said, "Sir, look at your feet. There is a fire below deck where we stand. The ship could easily blow up again. I think we should get off the ship now. Losing another life to save an insurance company some money is not my idea of a good plan."

We returned to the stern of the vessel and climbed down a rope ladder to a forty-foot boat, waiting to take us back to the *Heyer*. I filled my lieutenant in on what I had seen. He was the on-scene commander, and I left the bridge to let the two lieutenants come up with the next move. I returned to the bridge with three cups of coffee. I preferred bourbon, but it was not available during active duty. The lieutenants were bantering back and forth, and I said, "Sirs, can I make a suggestion?"

My lieutenant said, "Of course, Chief."

I said, "Sirs, I think we all understand that this is bigger than both crews of both our eighty-twos can handle. What we need is a 378-foot cutter like the *Rush* with her trained firefighting teams, but I know it is in Alaska. I know of no civilian outfit capable of handling this, but I do know of a well-trained outfit that is more than qualified."

"Chief, go on."

"Sir, the Navy has a well-trained group of men at the training center at Treasure Island, along with seagoing tugs. I think if the Coast Guard captain of the port of San Francisco was to ask them for assistance, they would be more than qualified to handle this."

My lieutenant asked me to leave the bridge, and I did so. Within minutes, the *Heyer* was underway, racing back to San Francisco and our mooring at Yerba Buena Island. It took about two hours, and as we went, the lieutenant was on the radio talking with the group office. As we ran under the Gate and back into the Bay, the lieutenant asked me if I had my dress uniform on board. I said, "No, sir, it's at home."

We tied up, and the lieutenant, after just a few minutes, came out of his cabin in his dress uniform. Just then, a vehicle pulled up onto the dock. The lieutenant said, "Chief, jump in."

The car took us out the station gate and up onto the Bay Bridge in the direction of San Francisco, and that was when I asked the lieutenant, "What the hell is going on?"

He asked me, "Chief, how certain are you of this Navy team you mentioned?"

"I've trained with them several times, sir," I replied. "They're the best."

Again, I need to go back a bit and explain.

In my Coast Guard career, I had the misfortune of being sent three times to the rigorous Naval Training Center at Treasure Island. The first two times were a true education. The Navy had built a makeup ship compartment that they called the *Butter Cup*, and it was something from hell. They would first set a large fire inside the compartment, and with the smoke, flames, and heat, you couldn't see anything but were ordered to put out the fire. And if your team was good enough to do it, you were ordered to take your oxygen breathing unit off to feel what it was like to be in a fire with your lungs burning. The compartment was then quickly ventilated, and it would come over the loudspeakers that your ship had just taken a torpedo hit and was taking on water. Valves were opened, and freezing cold water from the bay was pumped into the false ship compartment from all directions.

Our team was then asked to set up our dewatering pumps and try to patch broken pipes and holes in the sides of the compartment, and if we began to win the fight, more valves were opened up until we were chest high in icy water. It was made to be a no-win scenario.

My third time through the course was different, as it was meant to be. I was chief by that time and an observer with the chief instructor. We would talk about what the men in the course did right or wrong, which gave me a much more objective view of the experience than my previous two times as a participant. This was a school I was sure that I and many others would never forget.

The lieutenant and I finally arrived at the Coast Guard Marine Safety Office in downtown San Francisco and entered a conference room that just about scared the hell out of me. Attending was the captain of port, the district admiral, and many others. The meeting began, and the lieutenant brought everyone up to speed as to the ship still on fire anchored off the coast. Then, he looked at me, and with no warning, said, "Chief, would you give us your recommendations?"

I about swallowed my tongue. I was the lowest rank in the room. My tongue somehow loosened up, and I explained that I had been aboard the ship and then proceeded to detail the fire conditions I had seen on board. I told them it would take several fire teams to combat the fires I had seen on deck and below. "I don't have to tell you, sirs, the urgency of this situation and the environmental problems that can come as a result of this. There are no civilian outfits capable of handling this, and the cutter *Rush*, the only local Coast Guard crew that could, is away in Alaska. There is, however, an extremely qualified team of men at the Naval Training Center at Treasure Island. I have trained with them, and they are more than qualified." I was then asked to leave the room.

A few minutes later, the lieutenant came out and explained quickly that I was to report immediately to the Naval Training Center at Treasure Island. There was a car waiting for me. He was going back to the *Heyer*, and I was to keep in constant contact with him. As he said this, he handed me a radio set to channel 22, a well-known Coast Guard working channel. There was no hesitation at the Treasure Island gate, and soon, I entered the Treasure Island Training Center's front door, where I was immediately introduced to Senior Chief Walker.

He said, "We have all your required gear, Chief, and we will get acquainted as we go."

I don't know what it was about this man—his strength of voice, his tone, his outgoing nature—but I liked him right off. There were about two dozen men who I could see getting on board a navy sea-going tug. I followed Senior Chief Walker to the bridge. As we got underway, Walker looked at me and said, "I understand, Chief, that you requested my team for help."

"Senior Chief, I did." (I should note here that senior chief is a rank of enlisted man that most officers don't want to fuck with.)

"Chief, tell me what we are looking at."

I filled him in to the best of my knowledge and called the *Heyer* to let them know we were underway on the navy tug *Sea Wolf* and that Senior Chief Walker was in charge. The lieutenant came back saying that the *Heyer* would also be underway in a matter of minutes, minus the chief engineer. I understood this to mean that the XO and second mate were now aboard the *Heyer*.

Senior Chief Walker then picked up the radio on the bridge of the tug and shifted it to channel 22. "*Point Heyer*, this is Senior Chief Walker aboard the *Sea Wolf*." The lieutenant acknowledged the communication, and Walker said, "Lieutenant, I understand you are the on-scene commander. Chief Grayson has described what we are up against, and once I see what it looks like, I will deploy my men accordingly. And I will keep you informed." In other words, *Keep the fuck out of my way, and Chief Grayson is under my command to do with as I see fit.*

Senior Chief Walker looked at me and said in a strong tone of voice, "Any questions, Chief?"

I looked back and said, "No, Senior Chief. I think we have a job to do here."

"Let's go do it," he said.

It took another few hours to go down the coast and back to the *Puerto Rican*. It was still ablaze. Senior Chief Walker had the tug come up to the stern starboard side and hold while we all climbed aboard up a rope ladder. Then with ropes, we pulled the needed gear on board. The men quickly set up water hoses to the tug. Senior Chief Walker said, "Let's go, Chief."

I knew where he meant. He gave the go-ahead order, and a dozen men on two hoses began moving below into the ship. The hoses were charged with a retardant foam all from the tug. We all put on our OBAs (a complex oxygen unit used in such operations). We went below deck and couldn't see much of anything with the smoke and heat from the fires below. I was right behind Senior Chief Walker as we went below deck. He directed the fire teams by hand signals, and when visibility got too bad, he had a touch program (a form of tactile signaling) that his team understood. They pumped foam below deck and smothered the fires as we moved below. In almost total darkness, I followed Senior Chief Walker into this pit. Without his lead, I would never have been there. He moved the teams below and slowly put out the fires below deck. He then set a reflash watch, which meant to watch out for the fire reigniting from its own residual heat. We backed off the upper deck, and Senior Chief Walker directed the tug fire monitor toward the deck fire, and now the ship was just smoldering.

This experience created a lasting bond between the senior chief and me. In fact, we still talk today, as good friends.

The ship was under watch now by the owners and thought to be stable. Tugs and fuel barges were brought out to remove the unburned cargo, but a storm hit the ship and, with the action of the waves, broke her apart because of her weakened condition forward of the superstructure. As a result, the stern with the superstructure (some three hundred feet of vessel) sunk to the bottom of the ocean, while the four hundred feet of the bow was towed into the bay to a shipyard for scrap. The half of a ship still sits outside the city of Half Moon Bay, leaking fuel up onto its beaches, with little to be done about it. On the subject of marine pollution, there is a very interesting study conducted off the coast of San Francisco that should be read by anyone living along that beautiful coast where I grew up. The study is called "Beyond the Golden Gate: Oceanography, Geology, Biology, and Environmental Issues in the Gulf of the Farallones."

Chapter Twelve

DENISE

Whenever I could, I went back to the stables with Jerky and to take Chaser for a ride. Only, this Saturday morning was different. As I got out of my truck and headed for the barn with Jerky, meaning to take Chaser for a ride, I saw this girl I had never seen before riding in the arena. I stopped and looked, as any real man would do. She was a very pretty blond on a huge (sixteen hands plus) Appaloosa. I was watching her ride, and I could tell right off she was a good rider. Call me whatever you want, but there is nothing sexier than a pretty girl riding a horse and riding it well. Maybe it's just me. In any event, she stopped and walked her horse up to the arena rail where I had been standing and watching. I said, "You handle him very well."

She said in a very sweet voice, "No, he is a little rank. I've been away for the past week visiting my father in Alaska."

When I heard the word *Alaska*, my mind went into overdrive, recalling all the experiences I'd had there with the Coast Guard. Understand, I was and never had been a sweet-talking ladies' man. But this opened the door. Denise and I were married six months later and separated fifteen years after that. She lived three miles away, and I felt those three miles were getting closer every day. But this book was supposed to be about the Coast Guard, so let's get back to that story.

Chapter Thirteen

ALMOST LOSING THE HEYER AND ITS CREW

One day while doing paperwork (that was what a chief did and almost never touched a wrench anymore), we were getting reports over the weather radio of bad weather and building seas. You would think that everyone thinking of going out to sea would hear the same reports and stay safe in their harbor, but no. It was now late afternoon, and we got word that two thirty-five-to forty-foot cabin cruisers had left Half Moon Bay thirty miles south en route to San Francisco. Apparently, the sailors of both vessels were friends, and each ship had four to five people on board. Wouldn't you know it. Now they were calling for help.

Now, I might hear about this comment later, but I didn't think the group office that deployed our vessels had any idea of what they were doing. I was sure most of the office had never been to sea and had little knowledge of the coastline outside the Gate. Yet they made the decisions about which boats to send out. A good example of their incompetence was when we were ordered to get underway and go hide behind the Farallon Islands due to a possible tsunami that was to hit San Francisco in about one hour. We did as ordered, and after two hours, of course, nothing happened. We were then told to go to Half Moon Bay and look for damage. I looked at the lieutenant and said, "Sir, that is going to take us about four hours round-trip, when they could just pick up a phone and call the harbor master about any damage." Somebody in the office must have said this was an idea, we could just call down there because soon enough, we went home. In this case, they sent out a forty-four-foot boat after the cabin cruisers that hadn't gotten more than a few miles outside the Gate before they rolled over in the heavy sea. These boats were made to withstand a rollover, but in this case, its radio antenna was ripped off and one engine shut down, and it was lucky to be able to limp back into port. Next up was the *Point Heyer*. Someone must have thought, *An eighty-two-foot boat should be able to handle this*. So off we went. Now I need to explain a little about the coastline of San Francisco. On the west ocean side of the San Francisco Peninsula is a long beach, maybe ten miles long called, appropriately, Ocean Beach. It is very shallow off shore, and when you get any large sea state, it magnifies and builds huge waves in this area that can break much farther out than normal. These people had no idea of these charted waters or apparently how to listen to a weather radio, so here they were, a few miles off Ocean Beach, getting hit hard by large waves until one boat went over and all five people wound up in the water, holding on to a small life raft. The other boat had the smarts to turn out to sea and fight the oncoming waves until out far enough beyond the shallows so that the waves would become manageable. It then was able to turn north and get into the main ship channel entering the bay. Under the Golden Gate Bridge, the water depth was about three hundred feet, and the channel went out at that depth for miles until well out to sea. I believe this was due to the large riverlike currents that moved through the gate. It was easy to imagine the huge amount of water that flowed through the Gate, racing and lowering the water height of the Bay every twelve hours with a possible three-feet-tide change. As we were going out, just a few miles beyond the Gate, we came across the first boat limping in with a two-foot hole in its bow, taking on water. The lieutenant ordered the ridged hull rescue boat be put over the side and the people taken off the sinking boat. This wasn't easy in fifteen-foot waves, but our two men managed to safely make the two trips back and forth that were required to get all hands off the sinking boat and onto the *Heyer*. Talking about the tides of

San Francisco, I heard that boat landed days later on the rocks thirty miles north, near Bodega Bay.

The lieutenant carefully turned the *Heyer* around, which was no easy task in the midst of those large waves, and quickly headed back to port for an awaiting team of corpsmen. Our job was far from done after dropping our rescued people off at the station. We had five more people still in the water. We raced back out the Bay, but by now, everything had changed. The sea state had gotten bigger, now about thirty feet, and it was getting dark. We headed out of the ship channel and tried to round the point a couple of miles off the world-famous Cliff House, when the *Heyer* got slammed, hard. We had the searchlight on above the bridge, but you just couldn't see the monsters coming at us. I was holding on to the railing on the bridge and was scared to death as the next wave hit, and I could feel the *Heyer* barely recover. I was so terrified. I couldn't say anything to the lieutenant, but in the dark of the bridge, I watched the lieutenant swing the wheel of the *Heyer* completely around and gun the engines. The next wave hit at our starboard stern. There was a flaw, I think, in the design of the eighty-two: the rudders were too small, and in a churning sea, the boat could capsize. The lieutenant could also feel its movement and quickly following, pulled the starboard engine into full reverse and port engines full ahead until it slowly righted itself. We fought our way back into the bay and safety. The lieutenant picked up the radio and called the group office, saying, "I have turned the *Point Heyer* around and am returning to dock. I am not going to risk my boat or my crew any further."

This was the end of his career. There is a saying in the Coast Guard. "You may have to go out, but you don't have to come back." The 378-foot ship the *Morganthal* was sent out. It was a sister ship to the *Rush* and, as I had explained, very capable. In thirty- to forty-foot seas, it went out off the Ocean Beach and, with its power, was able to maneuver and position herself to be able to lower its twenty-four-foot ridged hull inflatable boat and pull the four people from the water. One older man was not able to hold on to the raft and died. In the captain of the *Morganthal*'s report, he said that the lieutenant of the *Point Heyer* had made the right decision to save his boat and crew. Adding that, had he persisted, we would have lost an eighty-two-footer and its crew. I was there, and I believed it.

The next day, we were told to be in dress uniform, standing by at the dock. The twelfth district admiral (meaning all of California) was driven down the dock in his staff car. He got out and walked up to the lieutenant, asking about the two men who had taken the rescue boat in high seas and successfully made the rescue. The lieutenant pointed the two men out, and the admiral pinned a lifesaving ribbon on each of their uniforms.

He then walked back to the lieutenant, and I heard him say, "Do you think I've forgotten about you and the rest of your crew, Lieutenant?" And he pinned a unit commendation on the lieutenant's uniform. That meant the lieutenant was soon to make the rank of commander. Many years later, I heard the lieutenant had made captain and was skippering one of our new 410-foot cutters. I would love to make one more trip to Alaska aboard one of those beautiful ships.

Chapter Fourteen

PORT CLARENCE

I need to jump back about ten years, as I jumped ahead about ten to finish the Anna White story, because there was a big part that I left out. I was second-class engineer and had been transferred from the cutter *Rush*, after my first two-year tour of duty on it, to the sweetest job I ever had in the Coast Guard. I was working for the Marine Safety Office in San Francisco. Our job, mostly, was to investigate oil spills and board ships coming into the Bay to check their manifest and cargo. I had more time off and was playing golf and trapshooting. The job was going great, until I got a call one day from one of my so-called friends at the office just laughing his ass off, saying, "I just got your orders, and guess where the fuck you're going?" After he stopped laughing, he said, "Port Clarence, LORAN Station, somewhere in the Arctic Circle of Alaska."

Yes, the Coast Guard has hellholes you wouldn't believe. There is a misconception that the Coast Guard only sails and patrols off the shore of the United States, but we do much, much more. It took a navy request to President Johnson to sign a mandate allowing the Coast Guard to leave US shores and assist on the rivers of Vietnam, taking control of port security there. I was going to recommend another great book for those with interest in the subject. This one was by CWO4 Paul Scottie, UCSG (Retired), and it's called *The Coast Guard in Vietnam*.

So I returned to the office the next day to get a hard copy of my orders. I had two weeks to set my life aside and report to the station seventy miles north of Nome, Alaska, for one year. That was easy; although, Jerky had six pups two days before I had to report. Luckily, my mother took care of the puppies, and a friend let me store my Jaguar in her garage. I slowly pieced it all together and was soon on a plane headed north. This was in February of 1977; there was no internet, no cell phones, and little radio or landline communication. I arrived in Nome and met up with my third flight, a small two-seat plane that was to fly me out to the station. As we came down, my first sight of my new home was barred in snow and ice. All you could see were some small wrinkles in the snow and ice that looked like barred buildings. A truck was there on the runway to pick me up and take me the final mile to the station. On the way, I saw a sign proclaiming this: "Population: Twenty-seven drunk and horny men."

I felt I might fit in here. That evening, as I was stowing my gear in a small room, I heard a commotion outside my room. As I looked out into the hallway, I saw a man in a woman's black negligee running past, with two men right behind who knocked him to the floor. Others came quickly, and the corpsman, who I had met earlier, pulled a needle and shoved it into the man's arm. The man went limp. The station chief, who I had also met, walked up and said, "This is no big deal. This guy freaks out now and then, but he is to be transferred soon."

Later, I went to sleep, or tried, thinking, *How could the Coast Guard allow this?* I found out the next morning that it was all a prank for me, as a newcomer. The lieutenant allowed these pranks so long as no one was hurt. In time, I took part in many of the pranks done on our newcomers.

The station was located at the tip of the Seward Peninsula, where, on a clear day, you can see Russian Siberia. The Bering Sea would freeze in jagged, rocklike formations of ice, and the Port Clarence Bay would freeze smooth so that it was travelable by dogsled or snowmobile. The station was located in this place for a reason. It was a LORAN station. One in a chain of stations around the world sending out a timed signal from its five-hundred-foot tower for navigation purposes, mostly for ships at sea. LORANs don't exist anymore now that we have GPS.

The temperature was generally zero and at times eighty below zero. In these temperatures, you had to wear goggles and wrap up to leave no skin exposed to prevent frostbite. I only once had to go out in that eighty-below weather. My good friend, Rodge, was clearing the runway that evening and ran the plow off the runway, where it got stuck. He radioed back for me to take the tractor out to the runway and pull him out. I wrapped up tight with underclothes, snow pants, and parka tied off with straps at the top and bottom. The tractor was open with no cab. By the time I got a mile out to the runway, I was frozen, and Rodge could see it. He helped me into the cab of the plow. There was no heat in the cab of the plow. There was no heat in any of the vehicles or equipment because nothing could warm up enough out there to put off the heat. Rodge set the chain and radioed Mike, "Put her in gear. I'm going to pull."

We got the plow out, and Rodge jumped into the cab, also freezing. After a few minutes, I told Rodge I would drive the tractor back into the station, and he should follow me with the plow. Rodge had always outranked me, but in this case, he agreed. We got back into the station where, again, Alex was waiting to check us over. We passed his inspection and knew how to do a slow body warm-up (it's easy to go from a cold hypothermic state and warm yourself too quickly so that you go into shock).

The importance of keeping the runway clear and landable in the worst weather was that we had the longest northwest runway in the United States. It was a boring daily routine to keep the runway in optimal condition. Beer was sold in small quantities, so one of my highlights of the week was on Saturday or Sunday, depending on the watch schedule. I would shove a couple of beers in the pockets of my parka, check out my pistol, and walk well away from the station to do a little shooting. I learned that beer freezes at twenty-two degrees and had to be drunk quickly or not at all. I had bought a real fur parka from one of the chiefs I knew before I left home. It was beautiful and warm, unlike the Coast Guard issue, but wearing it did present a problem. There was a pack of wild dogs at the station that lived mostly off our garbage, and they, for some reason, hated the Inuit people who would come by the station now and then. The dogs were not safe to pet but would not bother the men dressed in green standard-issue parkas. But when I stepped out in my fur parka, they would begin to growl. I had to take my fur parka off, lay it down in the snow, and they would come up and sniff me, and then everything was fine. The dogs attacked one Inuit man coming to the station, and just outside the front door, they tore him to pieces. We fought the dogs off him and got him into the station where the corpsman did what he could, and a medevac was called to take him to the Nome hospital. After that, the lieutenant ordered anyone going outside the station to be armed and in constant radio contact with the station. Most of the guys never left the station, but I did. I just had to go out walking or I'd go stir-crazy. I would check out my .44 and a radio and go. I had brought my big-bore .44 Smith & Wesson Model 629 with me. I was just not able to shoot the standard-issue military .45. But with this beautiful .44 that I had won at the second annual gun show in Valdez, Alaska, a few years earlier while serving on the *Rush*, I could and still can bounce beer cans at fifty yards all day long. I still have my parka and .44 and use them both from time to time.

We got a call from a bush pilot that he was flying in to drop off a new guy, but the weather was turning bad quickly, so he was just going to do a touch-and-go and back to Nome. This meant, *Here is your man. I'm gone.*

We geared up to go out to the vehicle bay that was heated. Our truck was down for maintenance, and the other was difficult to start. When it finely did start and we made our way out onto the runway, it was a whiteout. You wouldn't see ten feet in front of you. We creeped along the runway, stopping every twenty yards to yell and listen for response from our man. Eventually, we found him. He was sitting in the snow, just about frozen solid, hugging his seabag, with tears frozen down his face. You could only imagine how he felt, being dropped off in the middle of nowhere, in a storm where you couldn't see ten feet. We grabbed him up and took him back to the station, where the corpsman was waiting. Our corpsman, Alex, relisted the newcomer, John, the next, where he was immediately befriended by the whole station. No prank was needed here; he knew the reality of where he was, maybe better than most of us.

There were times when the weather got so severe that you would look up at the overhead as you woke up and see stalactites hanging from the ceiling from the moisture of your breath. A storm had set in, and for seven weeks, we were on our own. No flights in or out. We ran out of a lot of things. With no tobacco available, I quit smoking my two packs a day and was so hard up that I tried smoking ground leaves and whatever I could find. I began working out in our small gym in the boiler room and running our indoor one-eighth-mile main hallway that connected the station buildings. After the storm passed and a C-130 finally flew in with badly needed supplies, I tried smoking again and have not since. If you want to quit, it's easy; just go to the Arctic for a few months, and go insane.

During the Christmas holidays, the lieutenant took a week's leave and went home. The XO was a warrant officer and a hardcore alcoholic. I somehow got the job of putting together a list of who wanted what to drink during the holidays. The XO wanted four bottles of 151-proof rum. And the list continued; some of the men asked for pot or weed, and I had to tell them I couldn't help them with that. As I completed the list, I called into Nome on the radio phone and got the operator, who connected me with the local liquor store to put in our order. Then, I made another call to a local bush pilot out of Nome and asked him if he would like to join us for a Christmas party at the station. He said he would love to, so I asked if he'd pick up our booze order from the liquor store, and, of course, this was no problem. He would land on the runway, and both trucks were waiting. We would tie down his plane in case of wind and weather and assisted his passengers off the plane and back to the station where we could get better acquainted. The passengers were six young girls, about eighteen to twenty-two, and made friends easily about the station. The station, you might say, went into auto mode. The XO was rarely seen. Everyone who I knew of was standing their watches, drunk or not. We started a poker game in our small made-up bar, and the pilot sat in as the men would be sucking on 150-proof rum or 200-proof Everclear and dropping entire paychecks. I sat in and within minutes dropped $200 and said that was enough for me. Meanwhile, the girls were working the barracks. I didn't take part in that because I was in love with a girl back home (even though she couldn't remember my name and, as I found out later, was sleeping with everyone I knew, except me. I never said I was smart.) In the morning, walking down the hallway toward the bathroom and showers, I passed two naked girls talking just like they were passing down a major street in San Francisco, who paid me absolutely no mind. I was sure the pilot flew out with thousands from the poker table and his cut from the girls in the barracks. The lieutenant returned, and there was all hell to pay to bring the station back to normal operations.

About a week later, six men lined up in front of the corpsman's office to be flown out to the Nome hospital to receive shots and treatment for sexually treated diseases.

After being on the station for six months, I was allowed to take a week's leave and go home. It was, I'm going to say, unusual. I felt out of place. I didn't fit in with my family or friends. I didn't fit in, period. And after returning to the station, it felt different also. On the way back to the station, I, along with a friend, got stuck in Nome for the night due to the weather. We had a small room to stay in with the Nome armory. That evening, we walked down the road and entered the Board of Trade Saloon. As we entered, we could see an Inuit man flat, passed out on the bar and others drinking up a storm. The bartender shoved two men off their stools, and they hit the floor without any movement. He quickly wiped the bar and said, "Here are a couple of seats. What will it be?"

My friend and I carefully stepped over the men sprawled out on the floor and ordered a couple of beers. To say the least, we felt a little uncomfortable. After our beers arrived, my friend pointed out the pool tables in the back of the bar and suggested we go play some pool. So we moved off our stools so as not to disturb our friends on the floor and walked back to the pool room, only to find it occupied. A man had a woman on the table, and they were not playing pool. There were five others watching. We decided our game of pool would have to wait for later and immediately headed back to the armory.

We got back to the station the next day and went back into the same boring routine.

In the summer months, the bay and the Bering Sea would liquefy, with temperatures outside of seventy-five to eighty degrees Fahrenheit, but it was still uncomfortable to go outside due to the mosquitos. I had to get out, so I sprayed down in mosquito spray and covered my mouth with a bandana so as not to breathe in the mosquitos. I checked out my .44 pistol, a radio, and a few beers and started to hike down the peninsula along the beach. It was July 8, my birthday. As I got to the beach, the mosquitos began to diminish, so I could drop the bandana and pop a beer. As I walked a few miles down the beach, enjoying the sun and just being outside, I saw something in the distance. I was curious, so I continued on my way. I could now see large tents set up on the beach and a dozen dogs that were tethered to the ground and had now taken note of me and didn't look too friendly. I drew my .44 and walked at the water's edge, thinking I would back off into the water if one of the dogs got loose and shoot it if I had to. As I moved down the beach and saw three old wooden boats, about twenty-footers, it struck me that this was an Inuit summer camp. I had heard about these kind of camps from the Inuit in Teler Mission Village, some thirty miles inland, would set up temporary camps along the coast and hunt for seal and other game. I made my way slowly around the third boat and came upon an old Inuit man sleeping in the sand under the bow of the third boat. He woke up and slowly got to his feet. I noted three beat to shit rifles propped up against the boat. The old man said something I didn't understand, so I thought I would tell him who I was. I pointed north and said, "Coast Guard. Coast Guard."

He obviously understood. It turned out he spoke a little broken English, which made him smarter than me because I knew no Inuit, and I was in his land. We sat in the sand and talked. I understood most of what he said and learned that other men of his tribe were out hunting. I took my last two beers out of my backpack and offered one to him. I thought about this before doing it, knowing that the Inuit were highly susceptible to alcohol, but I thought, *How could one beer hurt?* We sat, talking and drinking our beer, when he said something I wasn't sure I understood. He said, "Do you want to see the polar bear?"

Then I started to think that maybe even one beer was too much. Even I knew that polar bears didn't come this far south. He talked slowly and explained that they had found this bear trapped on an ice flow coming down from the north, and one of their boats had found it and killed him. Again, he asked me if I would like to see it. I said, "Yes, Ishue, I would." (*Ishue* was the best I could understand his name was, and he called me *Muligel* for Michael.)

He led me into a large tent, and inside was a beautiful pelt of a polar bear tied off on a rack with the head still in place, looking down at me. It was like a cathedral, and I felt so sorry for this beautiful big animal. I walked up and touched its fur, which felt—I don't know quite how to put it—soft and fluffy, almost like silk. The old man and I talked a little more, and I realized I needed to get back to the station. I took the old man's hand and thanked him for sharing something with me that I would never forget. I made my way back to the station, and for several days, maybe even years, I thought daily of the old man and the sight of that polar bear.

We just happen to have a few beers with us to help
us wait for the snow-blower to pull us out. Out there
you have to drink them fast before they freeze.

Chapter Fifteen

THE REAL WORLD

I got my orders and left the station. Leaving an isolated duty station, you could just think about picking your next unit, and I did: back home to San Francisco Air Station. I look back at this and think I should have asked for Hawaii or someplace exotic and different, but at the time, I just wanted to go home to my friends and family. I was screwed up in the head from all the time isolated up north, and it took weeks to adjust to being back home. It was hard to explain just what was wrong, but suffice it to say that after a while, I adjusted and came back to what we called the real world.

I did little to nothing at the air station. At home I was shooting and racing motorcycles until I was badly injured by some stupid jerk who cut the course and broadsided me, breaking my leg in several places. My so-called friends put me and my bike into the back of my old truck and drove the ten miles out of the Montarra Hills and on into the hospital in San Francisco, stopping at several bars along the way. Thank you, Weasel, Bones, and Outs (you know who you are), and they never even brought me one drink. As I was in agony waiting outside some bar, they finally got me to the required hospital, where I spent the next three weeks getting my leg set and pinned. I spent the next six months in a cast. Afterward, the Coast Guard paid for all this, along with my normal pay, and stupidly said, "We will take him back."

They could have released me from duty due to the injury. Instead, I got orders to serve aboard the Coast Guard cutter *Midget*, another sister ship to my beloved cutter *Rush*. My leg healed well after the pins were removed and has always been strong. Even though the Coast Guard backed me up in many ways, and in particular when I was hurt, after eight years and making E-6 (first-class engineer), I left the Coast Guard. I went into commercial refrigeration, a field the Coast Guard had trained me in. Then, with some pushing from a friend, the Ozzy, as we called him, I took the tests with the Coast Guard for my commercial seaman's license, with a refrigeration endorsement. The Ozzy had been in the Seafarer's Union for years and sailed commercially for many years. He knew everyone and used his contacts to set up an appointment for him and me to meet with Mr. Lainson, the vice president of the Union, so as to bypass standing in line at the Union Hall, waiting for a job. The Ozzy said, "Bring lots of money because you are going to take us out to lunch along the wharf. Then you are, without notice, going to put $500 on Mr. Lainson's deck and say nothing."

I did as the Ozzy said. Mr. Lainson made a phone call and told me to be at Pier Nine on Monday at 7:00 a.m. to sail with the *Southeastern*. This happened on a Friday afternoon, so I had only about two days to prepare. In my life, I had always felt that someone was looking after me. My father died when I was twelve, and my older sister also died shortly thereafter. I had felt that they had been telling God on my behalf, "He isn't half bad. Give him another chance. He will do right."

Perhaps my father and sister were looking out for me that weekend because from nowhere, I got a call that Saturday from one of the chiefs aboard the *Midget*, who I barely knew. He said, "Mike, the Coast Guard is short on engineers, and in your case will pay you $16,000 to come back and sign an eight-year contract, plus $270 a month sea pay. You have not been out of the service ninety days, so you would retain your rank."

I thanked the chief for his call, poured a bourbon, and made a lifetime decision. Monday morning, instead of going to Pier Nine, I went to the Coast Guard district office that I knew so well and was signed up again and sworn in to protect the United States of America.

My orders came through immediately for a second tour of duty aboard the cutter *Rush*. Only, this tour of two years was not good. It was, I felt, a bad command from the top down, and I couldn't say any more about that.

I made chief and was supposed to be transferred immediately but was held on board for my thirteenth two-month patrol in the Bering Sea. But by this time, many things and people had changed aboard the ship. We had a new command, and you could feel the crew becoming more comfortable and working better together. I remember shortly after they came on board, the new engineering officer and warrant officer interviewed me about maintenance records and logs. I explained that I had nothing to do with the past engineering department outside of my own job under an inept chief. Then they explained why I was still on board, when I should have been transferred already. I was the only mental link they had to piece together a maintenance history of the ship. The new engineering officer and I talked often, and I filled him in on whatever work had been done on the *Rush* as best I could remember. Then we began to find shortages of engineering parts on board, and no records to account for them. Like I said, we just had a bad former chief, and it turned out he was even worse than I thought.

Chapter Sixteen

FLEETEX '83-1

We were to get underway for my thirteenth two-month Alaska patrol, but there was something else going on. I could sense a difference in the feeling on the ship. Once underway and picking up our helo out in the Bay as usual, we began to fall behind and follow the aircraft carrier USS *Coral Sea* out under the Golden Gate Bridge, as flowers fell from the bridge above. As we followed out to sea, other navy ships began to take up position around the carrier, and we did not turn north for Alaska as usual. Our new captain called for all hands not on watch to assemble on the messdeck. The captain came in, and all hands came to attention. There was a large chart placed behind him as he explained the first part of our voyage. We were going to make our normal Alaska patrol, but first we had been asked to assist in making history. We were to join the *Coral Sea* fleet and would later be joined with the *Enterprise* carrier fleet and the carrier *Midway* fleet. This would be the largest fleet in operation since World War II. Once assembled, the entire fleet was to skirt along Russian waters doing maneuvers, with which we would be involved in. And we sure were. To keep up with the *Coral Sea* fleet doing thirty knots, we had to refuel every three days. A large tanker would come alongside, moving about twenty-five knots, and shoot us a line called a messenger line. Then, larger lines were pulled across until the sixteen-inch fuel hose was pulled across and hooked up as both ships did a steady course, a few hundred yards apart. It was an unbelievable experience. Seeing the *Coral Sea* in the distance and its planes taking off and landing just as fast was like nothing I'd witnessed before. I could only imagine what it looked like from the air, seeing three incredible fleets sailing and somewhere, in the middle, was a small, white four-hundred-foot Coast Guard cutter, the *Rush*. As we approached the coast of Russia, our fleets were definitely on the Soviet's screens. I think the US told the Russians of our intent—to harmlessly pass by their country—because the next day, first thing in the morning, we had visitors. I didn't know much about this, but we had bears, Russian TU-95s, flying only a few hundred feet above the fleet with two US F-14 Phantoms on their asses. It was incredible to see up close. It had to be somewhat arranged because, as far as I know, we didn't allow vessels or planes within hundreds of miles of our carriers. These exercises went on for several days, and then the fleets disbanded, and we went our separate ways but not before receiving a message from the commander of the third fleet, commenting on the *Rush*'s performance:

> From: Commander, Third Fleet
> To: USCGC *Rush*
> Subject: FleetEx '83-1
> I commend the dedication and professionalism which you demonstrated throughout FleetEx '83-1. The smooth teamwork of all those involved reflects professionalism and dedication of which each member of the crew should take pride.
> Vice Admiral Sends

Somehow, our new captain arranged for the *Rush* to dock in the harbor of Kushiro, Japan, for four days. Kushiro is on Japan's northernmost island of Hokkaido. After World War II, the Russians demanded Hokkaido be theirs and were told absolutely not by General McArthur. This was a true experience. The small city of Kushiro had not been visited by Americans for many years. Before leaving the ship, there was a meeting on the messdeck with the Kushiro—I was going to say—police. They explained the currency exchange and, in a polite way, said, "Be polite and enjoy your visit to our country, and you will be well received."

And I found this to be very true. The captain shook hands with, I think, the police captain, and said, as he glared at us, "My crew will be on their very best behavior while visiting your country."

I had a wonderful time in Kushiro. The people were extremely nice, and I tried to show them the proper respect in turn. I took a bus trip around the island and found it nothing short of beautiful. As my travels in the Coast Guard brought me many places, I made a point of buying small dolls for my mother wherever I traveled. In this case, I found a beautiful doll of a geisha girl, enclosed in a glass case. And I continued throughout the years. Today, my mother has a collection of dolls from Japan, Alaska, and Mexico that she keeps under a sheet of plastic on display. We left Japan, and I felt in my heart that this was a place I would like to come back to someday. Given the kindness and civility of the people I met there, it amazed me that we were in such a brutal war with Japan not so many years before. We left Japan and headed toward Alaska to do our patrol on the Bering Sea.

We did our usual boarding of fishing vessels, checking their catch. Until, at the end of the patrol, we found the vessel *Yurimaru 31* underlogging its Pacific cod catch. It was seized and escorted into Kodiak for the state department to handle. We went home from a long two-month voyage. I finally got my transfer to the *Point Heyer*, which I had told of in earlier chapters, and then four years later was transferred to the *Blackhawk*, a buoy tender, and there isn't much to tell about that. We went up and down the California coast, just pulling up buoys and performing maintenance on them. After a year and a half on the *Blackhawk*, I got into a hardcore and down-to-earth conversation with my assignment officer in DC. I pissed him off by asking him what the hell land duty looked like. He hung up on me. I called back, and he said, "Chief, don't you ever talk to me like that gain."

I said, "Sir, I'm sorry. Can you please help me?"

He said, "Chief, I can see you have about twelve years' consecutive seagoing units and a year in the Arctic. I'm not familiar with the West Coast, but I do have an opening at the station in San Francisco."

I didn't know that he was moving me any farther than a few hundred yards down the dock to take over Station San Francisco and its five forty-foot boats, as chief engineers. I met with the outgoing chief, who was about to make warrant officer. He didn't tell me much, and later I found out why: He didn't know much. He was mostly interested in making rank and didn't give a damn about the boats and the crews. I also took a negative view and told my two first-class petty officers that they had the job. I was just there to retire. Once again, I was wrong. I could not deal with the mismanagement of the shop and the poor organization of the boats. I went to one of the boatyards across the bay to accept one of the boats leaving the yard after some repairs and a bottom coating. The work on the boat was supposed to be signed off on already, so I could just accept the boat. Instead, on my arrival, the boat was floating in the water, and no Coast Guard inspections had been made. I didn't know my way around the station yet, so I requested to see the captain. I explained to the captain what was wrong in my view. He made two quick phone calls, and the station lieutenant and the group of engineering officers were in the office in a minute. I didn't know that I had just jumped two chains of command by going straight to the captain. When I explained the boat was in the water with no Coast Guard inspections, the captain looked at the lieutenant and the group warrant officer and said, "I expect you to look into this. Chief, good work bringing this to our attention."

This statement from the captain saved me from catching hell for jumping two chains of command. The captain then said, in gruff voice, "I would like to know just how long we have been accepting boats from the yards with no inspections and paying for it. I will expect that answer in the morning, gentlemen." He stood up and said, "Chief, you continue with your good work. Gentleman, I will see you in the morning."

I didn't realize how much shit I had stirred up in my first three days at the station, but I was now untouchable.

I set up standards and responsibilities for all the engineers on the boats and had open group meetings with all my seventeen engineers every Monday, where we could all speak and share our points of view. Chester, my top first-class, was an outstanding organizer when given a free hand, and I highly recommended that he make chief on his evaluations. After a short time, this group of men and women made me look like I could walk on water. All it took was a little support and organization. And we had the best boats and crews in the whole Coast Guard. One of the boats was scheduled to have an engine change out, and we had received a rebuilt engine from an engine rebuilder whom the Coast Guard had contracted back East. My engineers and I rejected the engine and proved to the district group engineer that it was junk. At the Monday morning meeting, I was overwhelmed by the crew speaking out.

"Chief, why can't we rebuild our own engine?" I had no answer for that. I said to make some calls for parts, machining, and best estimate, and I would take it up to the captain and the district office. The final estimate, even with my 20 percent fluff, just to be right, was thousands of dollars less than the contracted junk engine. I took the estimate and time frame and spoke highly of the training value for my engineers of rebuilding an engine and presented it to the captain. The captain gave his approval and said, "Chief, now sell it to the district engineers. They will be funding this project of yours."

Even with the captain's approval, the district office took some convincing. Again, I spoke of the invaluable training and the result of a great engine more quickly and for less money than the contracted engine. The next day, we had approval. When I told the crew the news that morning, everyone was walking on air. Now let me explain: This engine was a 903 Cummins V8 turbo-charged engine—two in each boat. It was an engine about the size you might see powering an eighteen-wheeler truck down the highway. This engine was probably the most documented rebuild ever. Chester and I never touched it. The crew pulled it from the boat, brought it into the shop, and pictures were taken at every point of disassembly and reassembly. When parts were sent out to be machined and later picked up, I didn't send one person—I sent six. I had it worked out with the shop to show my people what they were doing. Let me explain why. Years before, when I was on the cutter *Rush* and we would go into a shipyard for repairs and upgrades of equipment, I found it fascinating to see these talented workers dry-dock the ship, weld on it, and oversee the required machining in the shops. I was sad to say there were few such talented workers in the US today, and one day it was going to bite us in the ass. As the engine came apart, Chester showed the crew how to take size readings of components being removed using a micrometer and other measuring devices. Chester was a damn good engineer. We had the group engineer walk into the shop twice a week to check our progress, and the district engineer would come in unannounced maybe once a week. They would come to me asking about the engine, and I would say, "I don't know. Let's see."

I would lead them out of my office and into the shop and say, "Ash or Sal, can you explain to the commander and me the status of the engine rebuild?"

Once, Sal grabbed a clipboard from the wall and said, "Sir, we removed the crankshaft yesterday, and here are its micrometer readings before machining. We will pick it up tomorrow after it is measured."

The district engineer asked, "We?"

"Yes, sir, six of us go to the machine shop each time to drop off and pick up parts."

He said, "Thank you, petty officer." Then he turned to me and said, "Six personnel? To pick up parts?"

"Yes, sir," I replied. "As I explained, this is not just about rebuilding an engine. It is also about the training. Would you like to talk to Sal some more or someone else in the shop? They know more about it than I do. It's the crew's project, not mine."

"Chief, I have seen enough, but I will be here to see the engine run."

"Yes, sir, that should be in two weeks, maybe sooner."

"Sooner, Chief?"

"Yes, sir, it seems some of the crew spend their off time in the evenings working on the engine. They've been keeping my first-class Chester jumping to keep up with their progress and making sure that everything is documented and done right."

It was about ten days later when the engine was in the boat and running. And we had quite the crew on board. The group captain, the district commander, the station lieutenant, myself, and the regular four-person crew. Chester and another engineer took engine readings as we slowly broke in the engine for just a few minutes before bringing it up to full power. I didn't know why our project caught top brass's attention, but it did. And I was proud of my crew for making it happen.

Months later we got word that the district admiral (for all of California) was flying in by helicopter and was to land in the center of the station on the parade grounds. The only orders we got were to make the station and boats look as good as possible as quickly as possible. The lieutenant called or a quick meeting on the second-floor conference room with all department heads to check on our status, as the admiral was due any minute. The first-class petty officer in charge of the station maintenance started by saying, "The stations is ready for his inspection, sir. We are just finishing mowing the parade field."

He looked down at his watch and then stood and looked out the window, overlooking the parade field. "Oh shit!" he said. We all went to the window to see.

"Oh shit" indeed. In perfect letters, in the tall grass, one of the men had written the letters FTG with the lawn mower. Everyone knew this meant "Fuck the Guard." Within two minutes, there were three men, including the first class, mowing the field as the admiral came within sight. He landed, got into a waiting vehicle, and left the station. Saying nothing, I followed the lieutenant down to the yeomen's office, and the lieutenant let loose, yelling, "I want seaman Endon off this station and out of the Coast Guard."

Chapter Seventeen

AIR STATION SACRAMENTO

I was there when the big earthquake hit San Francisco. I had crossed San Francisco Bay Bridge that morning going to the district office in Alameda, returned to the station, and went home about 4:00 p.m. As I was getting out of my car in front of my house thirty miles south of San Francisco, I felt the movement and saw cars jumping about and telephone wires swinging. I got back in my car and turned on the radio and learned what had happened.

I picked up my son, Josh, from day care, went home, called Denise at work in San Francisco, and was told she was on the way home. I called the station and was told it was an all-hands recall but not immediate and to come in or call the station when possible. I made my way back to the station about 5:00 a.m. San Francisco was completely dark with the exception of some fires in the distance. The Bay Bridge was under military control. The bridge connects San Francisco to the Yerba Buena Island where the Coast Guard station was located, and on the other side of the island was the naval base on Treasure Island, an artificial, man-made island. Both the Bay Bridge and Treasure Island were built for the World's Fair in the late 1930s. The bridge spans from Yerba Buena Island across the bay and connects with Oakland, and this was where the upper deck of the bridge had collapsed and fallen onto the lower deck of the bridge. The Cypress Freeway crossing through Oakland also collapsed and killed many people. It took a long time to get things back to normal. In many people's lives, things would never be the same again.

Despite witnessing the devastation of the quake firsthand, the risk of future earthquakes was not a deciding factor for Denise and I to sell our house and move to a twelve-acre horse ranch in the California Sierra Foothills, just outside Grass Valley. I would soon be able to retire from the Coast Guard, and it sounded attractive to move there. Only, our house on the coast sold much more quickly than expected. So for a year, I lived on the station, going home only on the weekends to go work on the ranch. I live there to this day, running a few head of cattle. Denise lives a few miles away, and we are still close and talk every day.

I took the test for senior chief and felt very positive of making it but changed my mind. I knew I would be sent to sea again, and I didn't like the idea of leaving Denise and Josh, so I put in my request for retirement. My assignment officer in Washington said I would get my recruitment orders in three days. Instead, I got orders to Sacramento Air Station. I called him back, saying this must be a mistake. He said, "It is no mistake, Chief, and you will be told of your duties when you report in."

Three days later, I reported in to the captain of the base. This was the beginning of May. Standing in front of the captain with orders in hand, I again explained, "Sir, I am a boat chief engineer, but I do know a little about aircraft engines."

He stopped me right there and said, "Chief, I will tell you why you are here. Chief, your record shows that you have a background in air conditioning. The Coast Guard has sent you to several air conditioning schools, and you have independently acquired your state contractor's license in the field. This is why you are here. I do not want to see you in uniform again until I tell you differently. In the next few months, it is going to get very hot here in Sacramento. We have a contract out for $350,000 for a new AC system to be installed in the operation's center right inside of the hangar, that I can see is nowhere near completion. I want you to befriend these workers, find out whatever you can about the delays and problems with this company, and give me weekly reports."

The one good thing about this new assignment was that I was only an hour away from home, Denise, Josh, and our new ranch. So I did as I was told, befriended the workers, and simply told them I was a contractor working on the air conditioning system on the administration left side of the hangar, which actually ended up being true. I followed along with one worker and another, asking questions about the system, and actually learned a lot in the process—including learning a lot of the company's shortfalls and shortcuts. They were now six months behind on completion. After two weeks at the station, I made my second report to the captain, explaining that the contractor was diverting workers to other outside jobs, slowing the completion of our project, and that I had found numerous things in the contract that were incorrect—like pumps that were to be renewed but had just been painted to look new. The captain called for a walk around the station, meeting with the Coast Guard contracting officer (who I knew), the contractor and a few of his people, and myself. The captain had told me to be in uniform from this point on. As I joined the meeting in uniform, you could imagine as they said, "If looks could kill." The Coast Guard contracting officer went through my eleven-page report step-by-step as we walked through the system. I didn't know the outcome of the face-to-face meeting in the captain's office, but I saw a lot more intensity in getting the job completed over the next few weeks. I still asked questions and was just told to ask the boss. So it seemed no one was talking to me anymore.

I changed my interest and began looking at the abandoned air conditioning system on the left side of the hangar. I didn't know who misled the command by telling them that this system was unrepairable, but I did know that their answer to this two years earlier was to spend $20,000 placing window air conditioning units in the windows of the administration offices. I spent part of a day troubleshooting the old system and putting in a request to spend $150 for a thermostatic expansion valve, a common valve in an AC system. I installed the new valve and started the system up; it seemed to be working great. The pressures were right, and the temperatures were right, so I let it run.

I walked into the administration office the next morning. Everyone was wearing sweaters, saying, "Chief, what the hell did you do? It's freezing in here!"

I asked them to give me a chance to balance the system and make adjustments, telling them they'd love it when it was 105 degrees outside. After a few days, I got the system running right. And the contractor finally finished up his job on the right side of the hangar, but on a one-hundred-degree evening, I got a call from the station that it was hotter than hell in the operation center. I drove back to the station and walked through the control room of the new AC system, which I now knew well, and found the problem. There was a time clock to shut the system down at 5:00 p.m. like an office building. But this was the US Coast Guard, and we didn't shut down. I adjusted the clocks, and the system was up and running normally in a matter of minutes.

Chapter Eighteen

RETIREMENT

The captain called me to his office a few days later and told me he was pleased with the outcome of the air conditioning systems and my work to get the admin's side up and working. Then he asked me if I still wanted to retire from the Coast Guard. He said, "I hear a senior chief may be coming your way."

I wish now, many years later, that I had said no. The captain asked me if I would like to have a retirement party on the station. I said, "No, sir, but, sir, I have never been up in a Coast Guard C-130 aircraft."

He smiled and said, "Chief, I think I can arrange that."

The next morning, I was put into a C-130 awaiting on the runway. The pilot was Lieutenant Sanders, my boss in the maintenance department. We took off and circled, doing two of what they called *touch-and-gos*—landing and taking off again in rapid succession. I realized this was justified as a training flight and not a joyride for Chief Grayson, but, in reality, it was exactly that. We then flew up into the foothills of the Sierra and circled my ranch at a low altitude. I could see Denise and Josh waving up at us. We turned and gained altitude and went up into the high Sierra Mountains and circled Lake Tahoe. The back ramp of the plane was opened. Lieutenant Sanders and I tethered ourselves and walked out onto the ramp. The plane was now flying only a few hundred feet above the lake as the lieutenant read my retirement orders as loudly as he could, to be heard over the engine noise. At the completion, he said, "Chief Grayson of the United States Coast Guard, you are now a civilian. As low as we were flying over the lake, I wondered for a moment if they planned to throw me into the water—one final prank. But soon we were in flight once more, returning to the station. I would never forget this incredible way to leave a service that I loved.

Chapter Nineteen

THE TRANSFER OF THE RUSH

One day, I got a call from an old shipmate Jon, whom I hadn't talked to in years. He told me about the decommissioning of our ship, the cutter *Rush*, and that it was sailing from Hawaii to San Francisco, actually Alameda, California, where I went through boot camp and was now the twelfth district command center for California. It was to be sold to the Bangladesh Navy. I told Jon that I would be there. I left the ranch very early and took Bodie with me in my newly acquired convertible two-seater BMW Z3. He loved it.

Soon, my loveable big Labrador began to whine, which meant he needed to pee. We had been on the road for several hours. I pulled off the highway into a restaurant parking lot. I let Bodie go down to the beach as I picked up my cell to make a quick call. When I hung up, Bodie was gone. I ran through the parking lot calling for him. A lady coming out of the restaurant said, "Your dog just ran past me into the restaurant."

I knew this wasn't good. As I ran toward the door, it opened, and two waiters had a hold of Bodie, dragging him out, and I could see him swallowing what looked like a piece of steak. I took him from the waiters, and one of them informed me that I owed one of the diners in the restaurant a lunch. I put Bodie back into the car and returned to the restaurant, where I was introduced to an older gentleman sitting by himself. I introduced myself as the owner of the steak-stealing dog and asked if I could join him. He agreed, and I asked him if I could have a couple of drinks, on me of course, brought to his table while he waited for his new meal to be delivered. The man's name was Alfred, and he was very friendly, especially considering that my dog had stolen his lunch. He told me how he watched this big, white dog jump up and grab his food from the plate with his front paws. He found it startling and afterward thought to himself, *That doesn't happen every day!* He asked for his dinner to be delayed a few minutes, and we walked out into the parking lot so he could meet Bodie. He petted him and told me that I needed to feed him more steak, and, chuckling, I agreed, if he would pay for it. Alfred proved to be a kind and understanding man. Bodie had introduced me to many people in his own way.

The next introduction was many years too late. I pulled up to the gate at what is now known as the Coast Guard Island in Alameda. I showed my ID and was asked what my business was on base. I told them I was invited to see my ship that I had done two tours of duty on be transferred. He came to attention and said, "Chief, proceed!"

I drove down the dock and could see two 378-foot cutters—my ship, the *Rush*, and a sister ship, the *Morganthal*. I leashed Bodie and started walking down the dock, when Bodie decided to make his next introduction. My heart went *thump, thump, thump!* as I saw her walking down the gangway of the *Morganthal*. She was in working blues and filled them out beautifully in all areas—blond and stunning. She stopped at the end of the gangway and started petting Bodie. After I collected some of my composure, I saw anchors on her collar and said stupidly, "You're a chief?"

She said, "Yes, electronics. Chief Moran."

She was still petting Bodie when I introduced myself as retired Chief Engineer Grayson. Then I just had to follow up with something stupid, so I said, "They didn't make chiefs like you when I was in." I bet she heard things like that a lot because she just smiled. I thought better of my last comment and said, "Chief, it has been a pleasure meeting you, but Bodie and I are late for the ceremony for the *Rush*."

She asked, "Were you on the *Rush*?"

I replied, "Yes, for two separate two-and-half-year tours!"

As I walked away, I had to look back. She was still standing in the same place watching Bodie and I walk away. I couldn't miss the large ring on her finger and thought, *What man could deal with her going away to sea for two months at a time with a mostly male crew? Maybe I should reenlist?* But that was just me daydreaming.

Bodie and I continued down the dock to a large covered tent-like area with many chairs set in front of the *Rush*. I saw my friend Jon, and we talked about old times on the *Rush*, and I asked him if he had made chief because we had both been first class on the *Rush*. He said he had made warrant officer. I said, "Maybe I should be calling you sir!"

He told me to knock it off, adding that he had paid dearly for his rank. He was sent to Washington, DC, for two years and had to leave his family back in San Francisco. It came to mind why I did not pursue the rank of senior chief myself.

At this point, I spotted an unexpected face in the crowd, one I hadn't seen in years: Ripley, who was also a boot on the *Rush* with me and who, years later, served with me at the station in San Francisco as chief. The ceremony began with words from the chief of staff for the US Coast Guard Pacific Area, then onto the US ambassador to Bangladesh. But what impressed me was something that the Bangladeshi vice admiral said: "The beautiful ship will be the pearl of the Bangladesh Navy." It was my pearl for many years.

The Coast Guard crew lowered the US flag from the ship's jack staff and marched down the gangway to the dock and came into formation. The Bangladesh Navy, in their colorful uniforms, then marched up the gangway in the high-stepping march and raised the Bangladesh flag on the jack staff. I said goodbye to my friends and promptly left. I was hurt to say farewell to the *Rush*—along with so many of my fellow Coasties.

Again, this was a point where the book could end, but I was going to make a statement I hoped you would understand after I shared one final story. Sometimes everyone needed a little a help, and sometimes you just couldn't take that feeling out of a coastguardsman to be the one to offer that help. Without a doubt, God had thrown many things at me that I just couldn't choose to walk around.

The next story was quite emotional to me—and again, completely true. I did twenty-five years working on commercial refrigeration on my one-man shop in Grass Valley, California, until I finally retired. My free time now went into trapshooting and fishing. One of my favorite fishing spots was Pyramid Lake, in Nevada. I had to tell you a little about the lake. It is on a Piute Indian reservation, and the indigenous inhabitants allowed people to come to their land and fish the lake for a small fee. Between the Piute and the State of Nevada's Fish and Wildlife Department, they had made an incredible fishing environment. High in the Sierra Nevada is the beautiful alpine Lake Tahoe and snowcapped mountains all around. At the north end of the lake, water leaves the lake, running down the Truckee River, winding down through the mountains, and eventually into the Nevada Desert and into the desert lake, Pyramid Lake. The lake is twenty-six miles long and in places as much as eight miles across. The landscape is desert and moonlike with its weathered rock formations. Yet in the midst of this seeming desolation, the fishing could be phenomenal. As beautiful as it is, I'm sure Pyramid is listed as one of the most dangerous lakes in the country. It could be sunny and flat-ass calm and within minutes, change to thirty-knot winds and four-foot waves.

I had my trailer parked along the upper camping area overlooking the lake, and my old eighteen-foot glass ski boat, which I had kind of converted into a fishing boat, sitting alongside. That morning, I had fished in the north end of the lake, and on the way back, I noticed the fuel level dropping fast. I got back to the dock almost on empty (though I still had my fifteen-horsepower outboard to get me back in if needed). I was planning on taking the boat home next week, but something told me to take it to the resort three miles away and put ten gallons in it. Just a feeling. It was late afternoon, and I was starting on my second drink, overlooking the lake back at camp, when I saw a group of people gathered along the beach. Then I heard it: One of those damned noisy Jet Skis. I was right: The fishing season was done. The group of people were taking turns on the Jet Ski, just going crazy. I tried to put it out of my mind and think about what I had to do the next morning to pack up and leave. I noted my flags (the American flag and a US Coast Guard ensign I'm very proud to fly) picking up in the wind.

As I was sitting there, it came to me that it was now quiet. *Thank God.* I looked toward the center of the lake, and I could see something indeterminate happening there. I grabbed my binoculars from the trailer, and I saw it: two people afloat near the center of the lake, about twenty yards apart, and the Jet Ski being blow away. I had gotten the lake weather report that morning: water temperature, forty-eight degrees.

I ran down to the beach, to the group of people who had no idea what was going on, and worse, didn't speak English, so that I could not explain to them the situation. I shoved my binoculars into a man's face and pointed out into the lake. He saw what I saw. I turned and pointed, saying, "Boat! Boat, now!"

He and another fellow ran up the beach, and I indicated to them to get into the boat as I started up my truck and drove as quickly as I could down the boat ramp to launch the craft. It was up to me to get it in the water; my new friends understandably didn't know what to do. I left the truck and trailer at the ramp and began racing out into the lake. I realized that I had my cell on me and called 911 for help. The operator came online, but I was so jacked up I couldn't speak clearly.

She said, "Settle down and take a few deep breaths, and then tell me your emergency."

I did as she said, regaining my composure, and said, "I am Chief Grayson of the United States Coast Guard. I have two people in the water in Pyramid Lake, between Pelican Point and Hell's Cove."

She said, "I am calling the Lake Rescue now. Keep your cell line open."

We had gotten to the middle of the lake, and I maneuvered the boat as close as I could to the first person. The two Hispanic fellows dove over the side and threw a young girl up at the aft ladder and onto the deck of the boat. They swam for the second person as I again maneuvered the boat. Again, they pushed another young girl on board and climbed up themselves. I took the girls, all ten to twelve years of age, and wrapped them in a wool blanket that I always kept on board. I recognized it immediately: The youngest was in shock. Near as I could figure, they had been in the water about forty-five minutes, and that was long enough. The youngest was glassy-eyed, teeth chattering, and unresponsive. I had seen our corpsman in the Coast Guard help people coming out of the freezing water, so I reached under the blanket and began rubbing her all over. Her skin was ice-cold.

One of the Hispanic fellows from the back of the boat took exception to this, thinking I was doing something inappropriate, and yelled at me. I quickly stood and—in a very violent manner—pointed to him and told him to shut the fuck up and sit down. I went back to work. My mind was racing, *What do I do?* I gave myself a time limit of about one more minute to try to bring her around, and then I would just run for the dock and help. Before the minute was up, her eyes began to clear, and my constant question, "What is your name?" was answered.

"I'm Angela, and I'm cold."

I said, "Yes, you are. The water is very cold. Who is this sitting next to you?"

She said, "This is my sister, Anna."

I said, "Angela, I want you to hug your sister to keep her warm," with just the opposite in mind. I wrapped the two of them tight in the blanket and yelled, "Hold on!" And I gassed the boat for the dock. Four men on the dock tied up my boat and two jumped on board with blankets and whisked the girls away toward an ambulance. I yelled after them that little Angela was in shock.

One of the men turned toward me and said, "You did a good job. We know what to do from here."

I stood there a little stunned and then began getting the boat back up on the trailer when a woman walked up to me and kissed me. I didn't know who she was, and I stumbled out the words "United States Coast Guard. It's our job."

I took my boat back to my trailer and poured a stiff one. Overlooking the lake, it came back to me that as I was racing back to the dock, I had reached down and touched Angela's face, and she had looked up at me and smiled, her eyes clear and alert.

I just won my lifesaving medal.

ABOUT THE AUTHOR

I think I have had a very exciting life working for the US Coast Guard for twenty years, a service that I loved. Besides the Coast Guard, God has confronted me with many challenges that I was not able to walk around. This book should be exciting reading and mostly true.